# VEIL OF TORMENT

## Also by March Hastings

# VEIL OF TORMENT

MARCH HASTINGS

CUTTING EDGE

ISBN-13: 978-1-952138-83-6

Published by
Cutting Edge Books
PO Box 8212
Calabasas, CA 91372
www.cuttingedgebooks.com

# CHAPTER ONE

S HE EMPTIED the last ash tray and glanced about the huge living room for something more to keep her busy. Dawn blended with the light from the chandelier, muting the color of her orange velvet gown. All of her ached from the ordeal of being sophisticated and charming to seventy guests. Once again she had lived up to her reputation well. But now Ivy wanted nothing more than to drop down on her bed and forget the acclaim, the admiration. At least for awhile. But she kept moving around the low modern furniture propelled by something stronger than her fatigue. It was the cold, compelling sensation of dread.

She heard Colin's footsteps. He came in from the kitchen and stood for a few moments beside the door frame. She tried not to see him, tried to forget, for one merciful moment, that he was here and that his arms would soon be around her searching for the response from her body she could not give.

"Dearest," he said in a voice low with tender feeling, "Must you do all this now?"

She heard him snap off the lights. She drew in a quick breath and held it as he came toward her. He placed his broad palms lightly on her naked shoulders.

"Ivy, you're trembling." His large, kind eyes filled with concern.

She tried to laugh. "It's nothing. Overwork, I suppose. Opening nights are always difficult." She lifted a hand to her throat and touched the necklace of diamonds. Colin's diamonds. Colin's apartment. Colin's money. His love had brought her to stardom quickly. Without him, she might still be struggling in third rate parts.

Ivy made it seem casual, the turning away from him and strolling to the floor length windows which looked down on the East River. But her insides churned and shook. She prayed for her strength to last so she could act out love and desire with Colin in his bed.

His breath on her neck ended all possibility of avoidance. She leaned back against the stiff shirt front of his dinner jacket. His hands moved along her ribs and upward, cupping her full breasts. She closed her eyes and tried to force herself into the mounting of passion.

"I love you," he murmured beneath her earlobe.

"Darling." She let her fingers slide along the back of his neck and into the short hairs which bristled over her polished nails.

How many times she had given herself to men, always hoping that one of them could succeed in breaking through the barriers of her memory. But with each disappointment, her belief in success dwindled. Now, after three years, her reservoir of faith was drained completely. There was only one man who could make her come alive. And some day it would come to pass that either she would put a bullet through Mike Devlin's heart or surrender to him her last shreds of decency.

Colin turned her in his arms. She parted her lips and received the tip of his tongue. Taking a little step closer, she pressed her long thighs, her belly, her chest to him. She submitted to his searching touch along her buttocks. A lonely fog horn probed the silence.

"Let's be comfortable," she whispered.

It was strain enough to endure this thing, why make it worse by standing up?

They went to the darkened bedroom. The scent of Colin's talc and after-shave lotions mixed with the stale odor of cigarette smoke. She tugged one end of his bow tie and drew it out from beneath his collar.

He kissed the tip of her nose while she undid his shirt. Then she pushed him gently away. He sat down on the bed and waited for her patiently. The patience, the goodness, the consideration, she hated him for these qualities. She had grown to hate every man who could not free her from the image of Mike.

And while she hated him, she proceeded to take off her clothes. The expensive gown fell to the floor and she stepped out of it, revealing the matching orange strapless and pantie girdle. Colin could not stop looking at her.

For effect, Ivy sauntered about the room, dropping her earrings on the dresser, undoing the garter hooks. She stopped in front of the mirror and took the pins out of her chignon. Flicking her head sent the heavy blonde tresses cascading down beyond her shoulder blades. Slowly she unhooked the brassiere, knowing that Mike wouldn't wait this long for her. He'd tear the clothes off her and possess her on a chair, on the floor or wherever they happened to be. Possess her, that is, if he weren't stupified with alcohol.

Finally she stepped out of her high, silver heels and came to the bed. She put Colin's face to her belly and leaned over him. She had every reason in the world to be grateful, to feel secure and cherished. It was her own fault that they were still not married. She had thrust away all chances for marriage, knowing that her addiction to Mike would crash through her prestige and drag her reputation into a scandal it could not withstand.

Resignedly she sat down beside Colin and swung her legs up onto the mattress. She lay back onto the pillow and shut her eyes. As his lips grazed into the curve of her throat, she pleaded with her body to give her just one sign of promise. One little clue that perhaps she might live as other women lived.

Colin's mouth searched and probed and found her nipples. He worked her body with facile knowledge. Any normal female would be grateful for his attention.

His chest had begun to perspire. She felt their skin sticking together. Automatically she signalled him to move up on top of her. She arched her back and worked her hips. Grunts tore from Colin's throat. She dug her nails into his back and drew long red marks on his skin.

When Ivy felt his convulsions, she met them with her own. Someday, somehow, her pretense would be found out. She felt certain of it. Then the niggling whispers that Ivy was a fraud would claw away at her pedestal. The passionate actress would be unveiled as a frigid bitch. She did not want to think of this any more than she wanted to think of Mike. Doom seemed to be circling around her like a waiting shark.

She saw Colin fall back onto the pillow, exhausted. He smiled languidly through his reddish lashes. "When are you going to marry me?" he said.

Ivy reached across and squeezed his hand. She felt ashamed of her cruelty, but powerless to help either herself or Colin. "When I'm absolutely sure that I'll be good for you."

She had to spend another hour being cozy and affectionate before it was safe to leave him. He clipped out her press notices and slid them carefully into a manilla envelope. She took the envelope and rode down the elevator, realizing that she was no longer simply Ivy Sherwood but IVY SHERWOOD, on whom all the eyes of the theater world would be focused. She knew how cold those eyes were, how they watched every breath, every movement. She knew also her duty to Colin and to her press agent. If she wanted to maintain her career, build and broaden it, there was no room for personal nonsense.

She waited under the canopy while the doorman got her Lincoln. The distant sound of church bells tolled a peaceful morning for those who could believe in God. What could she believe in except ambition? It was all she had between herself and a beggar's life with Mike.

Her white convertible sped cross-town through the deserted streets. A hint of Autumn tinged the air, painting bright shades of reds and yellows on the trees of Central Park. She really should go home, take a bath, get some sleep. But the automobile seemed to move with a life of its own, heading downtown on Seventh Avenue.

Through the exhaustion stirred her twisted need to be with Mike. It rose in familiar torment, pulsing in her breasts and clutching at the muscles of her stomach. For a month she had resisted the impulse to be with him. She laughed bitterly, realizing that her good sense could manage to protect her for a whole thirty days. As she pressed harder on the gas pedal, wild phantasies occured to her. Dreams she knew could never happen. But for the moment she permitted herself to lapse into believing. Believing that her new gained wealth could buy the kind of surgery which hadn't been perfected yet. She could never think of Mike as a blind man. His rugged, dark-skinned body sitting helpless, useless behind thick spectacles. His black eyes still looked as sharp and bright as the day they had met. Only when he reached for a match or a glass did the fumbling touch betray his sightlessness.

Ivy cruised around the crooked streets of Mike's neighborhood, looking for a space long enough between the parked jalopies for her car. Still, she had to walk three blocks to his house, ignoring the curious glances that followed her clinging gown. How long could she get away with visiting Mike before squibs began to appear in the gossip columns?

Four flights up the worn steps brought Ivy to his door. She turned her key in the lock and stepped into the narrow foyer. The apartment had become ridden with scraps and bits of things during the period of his waning sight. Now she saw that the photographs of the buildings Mike had designed were taken down from the walls, revealing stark squares of white in the dirty gray.

Her narrow heels clicked on the wooden floor. She came into the small living room and found him asleep on the sagging divan. He lay dressed in a blue denim shirt and old dungarees. One arm lay across his forehead as though even in sleep he must hide from the futility of darkness.

She sat down beside him and touched her lips to his. Instantly his arm stiffened. The hand reached forward and caught her cheek.

"Oh, it's only you," he sighed.

"Only me."

He cleared his throat and sat up, scratching the stubble on his jaw. Then he folded his arms in a motion that told her plainly he didn't want to touch her. "How now, brown cow. Congratulations."

"You know?"

He had fits of interests in her career followed by intense boredom with it. She wished he was bored with it today and so lessen the contrast between her own success and his failure.

"I understand you had the critics weeping in their Martinis. That's my little poison Ivy."

Mike was staring straight at her and she sensed that he could somehow make out her form. Only two months ago, he could still tell the difference between light and dark.

She started to say: I wish you'd been there. But she choked off the words. Mike would never allow himself to be viewed where rich and successful people could pity him. Then it occurred to her that Mike had learned about her success rather quickly. She wondered how.

"Yes, I was pretty fortunate," she said. "Do I get a kiss for luck?"

"Ivy Sherwood needs luck?" He chuckled without malice. "If I remember correctly, a voluptuous shape, sky blue eyes and golden skin are all the luck any woman deserves to have."

She blinked to clear her blurring vision. He did still love her. He loved her as much as she loved him and he carried the picture of her inside his mind, distinctly and cherishingly.

Without shame, she leaned forward and put her head on his chest. Then she reached up and folded his arms around her. He did not resist her overtures as she kicked off her shoes and snuggled beside him. With both hands, she tilted his face down and lifted herself till their lips met.

Sparks shot through her flesh as she clung to him. Every nerve tensed and yearned for completion with Mike. Here in his embrace she was a normal woman seeking the fulfillment which was her right. The odd pieces of her private world tumbled into place when she yielded to his special rough caress. Dreams of stardom faded. The world of money and fame floated away out of view. For this instant, she was a willing slave to this angry, embittered man. Glady she would give up independence, family, self-respect to remain with him.

The hall door opened. Ivy heard another set of footsteps in the foyer. Mike pushed her away from him as the sound came closer.

"Well, aren't you up bright and early." The woman spoke to Mike with a certain possessive tone in her voice that set Ivy's teeth on edge.

Ivy straightened the bodice of her gown while she inspected the hard features glittering at her from behind too much make-up. Mahogany red hair frizzed out around her too thin face, emphasizing the protruding cheek bones and bony nose. A soiled cotton dress hung from her thin shoulders and fell unevenly about her spindly legs. She was hardly Mike's type ... if Mike could see.

From a brown paper bag, the woman produced half a dozen eggs and a package of bacon.

"What'll it be this morning," she said, continuing to ignore Ivy. "Scrambled or sunny side up?"

Mike groped to where his glasses lay folded on a small table beside the divan. "Scrambled," he said. "And Hilda, will you make coffee for two?"

"Who's the other one?" Hilda challenged.

Ivy felt her back stiffen.

"Try keeping your temper to yourself," he answered gruffly.

Ivy knew Mike was making an effort to shield her. She watched him fit the glasses carefully over his ears, the male strength vibrant in even his most delicate motion. With the appearance of Hilda, he had suddenly remembered that he could not take care of himself. But he would not let anyone else share the pain of it, or help him.

Ivy kept her silence till Hilda had padded into the kitchen. "I could have made breakfast for us," she said.

He patted her shoulder. "Sure you could." A hint of a smile twinged on his lips. "But she's dependable."

It felt like a smack in the face, but Ivy had to admit that he was only speaking the truth. They had fought this battle out a hundred times. He would not let her become a drudge in the service of an invalid. And in the acting profession, she could not be at his beck and call. The situation between them was too complicated for their lives to run smoothly. Anger and fear and love and futility tore them apart and threw them together again.

"I think you'd better go now," Mike said.

"Why, for heaven's sake?"

He shrugged. "Three's a crowd."

"You don't mean to tell me ..." She could not finish the horrible thought.

But sounds of triumphant humming emerged from the kitchen to complete the thought for her.

So it had come to this during the month she was on the road. Ivy wasn't really surprised, after all. She had wanted to cut herself off from him. She had promised never to come back after their last fight. And Hilda was part of his method to shut her out of his life. Frustrations of body and soul choked in her throat. She had no right to interfere with Mike's decision. Yet she could not tolerate the thought of her man making love to a person like Hilda.

Her man. Did she have a marriage ring to prove it? Did she have promises of undying love? All she had was the wild aching of her heart and the wilder craving of her body which brought her back again and again to this man who could not accept her.

Shakily she reached over and got her shoes. "Goodbye, Mike." Her voice held no conviction.

She tried to get past the kitchen without seeing Hilda. But Hilda poked her head out and tapped her on the arm. "You got a familiar face," she said. Her forehead wrinkled with the effort of concentration.

"Yours is pretty common too." Ivy couldn't resist the jibe, though she knew the woman wouldn't understand it.

She hurried outside and clattered down the steps, anxious to get away from the dismal thing that Mike was doing to himself. But she knew there was no place in the world far enough away so that Mike's fate would not touch her own.

# CHAPTER TWO

S HE RACED the car homeward, shooting past red lights and not caring. The manila envelope slid onto the floor and lay there unnoticed. She felt paralyzed in the grip of a depression which dragged her to new depths. Her glamorous exterior remained aloof from years of training and she felt grateful for this, at least, now that she was going home to her family.

Her fingers were too shaky to bother searching for the key and she pressed the doorbell.

"The prima donna," her father said as he opened the door. "Colin is phoning every ten minutes wondering what became of you. If you wrapped yourself around a lamppost in the excitement." He spoke with the genuine concern of a man who could not understand the mysteries of theatrical success and was anxious to stay clear of it.

"Let her be, Abraham. She heard enough voices for one night."

Ivy managed to smile for her mother's sake. "I went for a ride," she said steadily. "Is that all right with everyone?"

"It's not all right. A daughter has a business ..."

"Please, Dad."

The note of pain in her voice silenced him. She rushed off to her bedroom and closed the door, needing refuge. They had been a close family once upon a time. In the days when she had behaved according to her father's code of morals. She wished she had the courage to move out into a place of her own. But the emptiness which Mike left in her heart needed to be filled with something. And the love of a family, even a family which couldn't understand her, was better than the echo of her own loneliness.

Maybe now, with all the money coming in, she would get herself an apartment and a secretary. That way, she could pull a veil over the indecencies which filled her life.

She took off all her things and went to sit in the bathtub. Her head ached dully and she closed her eyes as the hot water soaked up around her. Despite the arguments, it was good to be home. The consolation relaxed her somewhat. She got her brother's terry cloth robe off the hook and tied it around her. Then she padded barefoot to her bed and fell asleep on top of the covers.

It seemed but a moment later that someone was shaking her awake. Her eyelids grated open and she smiled at Leo's pink cheeks.

"You better speak to him, Sis, before the house explodes."

She nodded and took the phone on its long extension from Leo's hands.

Colin was willing to believe anything she told him. She kept her story simple, telling him the truth by omission. It was easy enough for anyone to understand that she would want to go for a ride by herself at such a time in her life. He did not press the issue when she declined his offer to go out for dinner. Yes, he would pick her up and drive her to the theater tomorrow.

Leo took the phone and set it on the floor. Then he bounced on the bed and crossed his legs under him. "Say, you're top banana now, aren't you?"

The way he said it made it very important and filled with prestige.

"I guess so," Ivy admitted. She went to the dresser and began brushing her hair upward from the nape of her neck.

"Then you won't have to hang out with creeps like him any more, will you?"

She glanced at her brother between the strands of her hair. His innocent face asked the question with a directness that required a direct answer.

"Yes, I will," she said.

"But why? You can do anything you want, now that you're a star. I don't see why you still need him."

Ivy parted her hair and began to braid it slowly. "I wish it were that simple, Leo, but it isn't. A star doesn't shine all by herself in the sky. I'll always need the right people to say the right things for me, honey."

Leo shook his head. "Geez, that's tough."

"Yes, it's tough."

"Oh well, at least you're rich." His face brightened. He swung off the bed and headed for the door. "Don't forget," he winked, "to save some for poor relations."

Moments of shared confidence like these and moments like last night when the curtain rose again and again to thundering applause were the only things Ivy had to keep her steady. They made her remember that somehow, in some way, she was still managing to be a worthwhile person.

But it didn't kill the gnawing ache in her thighs. It spread savagely now, entwining her and consuming all the good intentions she had of spending this one day with her family. It was no use realizing that she could not kill the feeling anywhere except in Mike's arms. She had to keep trying, different men, different sensations, until something fulfilled the craving at last.

She put on fresh underwear and slipped into a plain wool skirt. Even ordinary street clothes showed the curves of her body to advantage. It seemed a terrible trick for her to look so willing and be so unable.

The odor of fresh coffee perking floated in from the stove. She put on flat sandals and went in for breakfast, knowing her mother had intuitively prepared breakfast though it was four o'clock in the afternoon.

Leo straddled a chair and concentrated on lacing a football.

"Nice wheat cakes?" her mother said, turning them over in the pan. Her yellow print apron extended starchily.

"Perfect," Ivy answered, mustering a show of enthusiasm.

The rustle of newspapers told her that her father was hiding behind world events in the living room.

"Don't mind him," her mother said, pouring coffee half way in a glass and adding milk till it reached the top. "He doesn't know how to show that he's proud of you."

I'll bet, Ivy thought.

She sipped the warm mixture and discovered that her stomach was really empty.

"We're all proud of you. You worked hard, you had determination." She twisted the narrow gold ring on her finger. "How many mothers can say: my daughter is Ivy Sherwood?"

The stubborn pride became suddenly unbearable to Ivy. She wished her mother would call her a whore and be done with it. Carefully, she finished the pan cakes, determined not to let her guilt flare openly. Then she carried her dishes to the sink and washed them.

"Pretty soon we'll have a cook and a butler, won't we, Sis?"

"Butlers, my eyeteeth," her mother put in. "Nobody's so lazy around this house except you. Butlers!"

Ivy stacked the dishes in the cupboard, wondering if her mother could be comfortable anyplace but in this old-fashioned apartment. Gladly would she get them a huge place overlooking the water or a rambling house in Long Island. Then her thoughts spluttered to a halt. Would they take the money she earned in the way she earned it?

Confusion piled on top of confusion. She must thrust her family's standards back onto the out-dated shelf where they belonged. Success could be important. It *was* important, whether they believed it or not.

She went to the closet and got a leather sports jacket which she flung on over her cardigan. "I'm going out," she said flatly.

"What, again?" Her father's voice came from over the paper. "Run in circles. Go ahead, run. Run. Some day you should get married already and bring children into this world."

The challenge was too much for Ivy. "What for?" she blurted. "So you can yell at them and stifle them too?"

"Aha. A loud mouth she's developing. Go. Go to hell if you want, my big star on Broadway."

His unfairness washed over her, burning acidly. At twenty-two he expected her to be married and in her second pregnancy. She wanted to scream that if Mike were well, she would be married, and pregnant, and respectable. But no one in this house would understand this. Sex must creep beneath a dark blanket.

She slammed out of the house and strode along First Avenue, pushing her way between the crowds of visitors emptying onto the street from nearby hospitals. Where she was going didn't matter, so long as it was away from the narrow mindedness and away from her troubles.

The blocks fled beneath her rapid stride. Her braids bounced defiantly. She caught a reflection of herself, grim and unhappy, in a grocery store window. The glamour stripped away, revealing the raw meat of frustration and desire. She had neglected to put on lipstick and her naturally red mouth pouted and drooped. Her eyes shown with a queer light combining tension and craving in two burning points.

At Twenty Third Street, she stopped and waited for something to happen to her. Anything. But let it happen quickly.

She stared at the marque of a movie house. On impulse, she bought herself a ticket and went inside, making no pretense to herself that she was going to see the picture.

She climbed to the balcony and sat down in the last row, looking for someone as lonely as herself. The world was full of perversions that she had never tasted. Perhaps one of them could satisfy her just a little. She crossed her legs and swung her ankles restlessly, puffing hard on a cigarette, unconsciously attracting attention to herself. The old men who eyed her she discarded as possibilities for the kind of relief she wanted. A sailor pushed his hat foreward to his eyebrows and popped a Cracker Jack into his mouth. She discarded him also. He was too young, too healthy for the miseries she had to offer.

The first feature ended. She had gone through half a pack of cigarettes. Nicotine coated her teeth unpleasantly. She got up and moved half a dozen rows further down. She waited. There was no place else to go anyway.

A voice behind her said, "Pardon me, may I borrow a match?"

Ivy turned and gave him the book of matches. She smiled at him, knowing very well that he had matches in his own pocket. But she appreciated the line. It helped them both preserve a little something of respectability.

In the dim light he looked neither old nor young. Just very tired. There were little dark pockets beneath his eyes which made even his smile intense.

A match flared. She saw the strong curve of his nostrils.

"Thanks," he said, handing them back to her. "It's a pretty bad picture, isn't it?"

If she weren't on the make, she would turn her back to him in a natural movement of dismissal. Instead, she rested her arm on the empty seat beside her and faced him diagonally.

"Yes," she said. "I was just thinking about leaving."

Without further comment, she got up and made her way slowly out to the aisle. As she walked down the steps, she felt his presence behind her.

A rush of silent protestations filled her at the idea of what she was about to do. Was she mad, picking up a stranger like this? Wind up dead in an alley. Or get a disease. All of her revolted against the action she was about to commit. All but the empty feeling in the pit of her stomach. A desire so insistent, so barbaric, that she was not free to choose between right and wrong.

She glided down the steps, listening to the squeak of the stranger's steps following her.

And suddenly she stood in the daylight again, on the sidewalk, looking up into his ageless, weather-beaten face.

"I guess we think alike," he said and put his hands into the pockets of his cord trousers.

"I guess we do," she admitted. He had gray-green eyes which reminded her of the sea around New England.

"Would you like to … go for a soda?"

She nearly burst out laughing in his face. Why make it so clean, so prim, this thing that was happening between them? Why make it decent, normal, the thing that would inevitably happen? But she didn't laugh. She felt touched by his efforts to allow her to play the role of a lady.

They strolled for a block or so till he escorted her into an ice cream parlor. Kids in their Sunday best were crowded into booths, telling jokes and playing with their bent straws. Nobody seemed to notice that Ivy Sherwood had entered. She wondered how many days of this precious anonymity were left. How long before her private sufferings would feed the smut hungry columns of voracious journalists.

The stranger led Ivy to a comparatively isolated booth in the rear of the store. She slid along the red leather and adjusted her jacket over her shoulders. The sweet odors of syrups almost convinced her she was in bobby socks again and that she had a right to be here with the man holding out a menu toward her.

"The name's Wilf," he said. "Scandinavian. You know, like Leif Ericson and those boys."

Yes, it was right for him, the name. He looked like he'd travelled a long hard journey, searching for whatever it was people searched for. And there was something about the shortness of his hair cut, shaved up high above his ears, that held a flavor of the European.

"Ivy," she said, "As in poison ivy." Mike had a way of putting himself between her and other people, even when she wasn't consciously thinking about him.

"I wouldn't say that." Wilf pulled out two paper napkins, putting one in front of her and the other in front of himself. "Poison ivy grows in the country, away from people. But you grow toward them."

She felt herself growing red from the sincerity of his reply.

A waiter came up to the table, saving her from having to cope with the unexpected compliment. They ordered ice cream sodas and Wilf got change from the man, putting the handful of silver into the small juke box on the wall beside them.

Ivy pressed the various plastic buttons, purposely choosing music that was lively and brash. She didn't want hearts and flowers to decorate her motives for being here with Wilf. Let the nastiness come out in the open. Let her sex urge sit bright and leering where he could see it and not deny it. She wasn't going to pamper him with a phoney flaring of romance. They were two animals slavering at each other because neither of them could handle the responsibilities of true love. Or its suffering. They were male and female anesthetics, offering one another brief oblivion.

Ivy sucked the chocolate soda up the straw, blotting out all the nice words with which Wilf was trying to amuse her.

Once more, they stood out on the street.

"Do you live around here?" Ivy said quite bluntly. She did not drop her glance or flutter her lashes. She did not smile nor insinuate with her lips. "I'd like to go someplace where we can really be alone."

She heard him draw in a breath and saw him purse his lips for an instant. "Yes," he said, meeting her own frankness. "My place is a couple of blocks down the street."

"Well then?"

"All right."

They covered the short distance without speaking to each other. The fancy dress of conversation was no longer necessary.

He steered her into one of the newer buildings put up between ancient tenements. His apartment was on the ground floor. She went directly to the windows and shut the venetian blinds. It was a pleasant, white-painted room, sparsely furnished but neat. Tones of brown gave a soft feeling which was warm without sacrificing masculinity.

Ivy noted that a foam rubber couch doubled for a bed. She sat down on it and pushed her jacket off.

"Come here," she said.

He approached her and she pulled him down beside her. Automatically, doubts of success began to pound inside her. A clammy film broke out on her skin. Yet she put her arms around his back and pulled him to her hard. It was like running blindly into destruction, just as a bull thunders at the elusive red cape.

Her insides screamed and flared. It had to happen for her. It had to happen.

She tore his clothes off and pulled at her own savagely. Her ears roared and her lips burned. A tremendous pulsing convulsed her thighs. She straddled his hips and put his hands on her own fleshy behind. Obscenities spat from her, but she did not hear them. All of her focused on a single goal toward which she raced desperately.

Mike... Mike... Mike!

Her head spun dizzily as she tried to hide from the thought of him. The couch squealed and groaned. She rocked forward and bit her teeth into the cheek of whoever it was lying beneath her. Perspiration rolled down the inside of her arms. She was out of breath and pain stabbed in her chest as she kept on flinging herself against the unyielding barrier.

At last she felt the sudden quivering of her nerves as when a taut string comes loose from its mooring. The quivering fluttered for awhile and then came to a dull stop. Ivy opened her eyes, knowing that, once again, she had failed. Her passion lay crouched inside her, lurking with bright hungering eyes. There was nothing she could do that would reach out and choke it to death.

She fell down beside Wilf and stared blankly at the spray of freckles on his shoulder. He moved toward the wall, as though knowing with instinct that her helplessness took up more room than her body.

They lay silently for awhile. Then he inched his way around her and pulled on his trousers. He went to the portable refrigerator and brought back a container of orange juice and a glass.

Ivy pushed the offer away. Already she had forgotten Wilf. He did not exist for her anymore. A ghost making longer the interminable line of ghosts that peopled her life. With robot fingers, she hooked and buttoned her own clothing.

Without saying goodbye, Ivy walked out of the apartment.

# CHAPTER THREE

S HE SHOULD go home. There would be telegrams and phone calls overflowing from last night. Important people whom she could not afford to ignore at this early stage of her career. The emptiness of her personal life felt too painful to dwell upon. If there was any salvation, it lay in work, ambition and more work.

A taxi drew up for a red light and she hurried into it, responding to her strengthening voice of self-preservation. The voice admonished her in steely tones. Her profile became rigid and imperious. Beneath her skin a mesh of fine wires held her together. A sensation of bloodlessness replaced the yearning. She slipped her wrist through the loop of the car strap and silently damned all men. And she damned Mike the hardest because he was responsible.

She lit another cigarette, mentally closing the lid over the lost, frightened core of her being.

When she got home, she walked in on Colin, trying to hide his agitation by sipping a cup of tea. His presence did not surprise her. No doubt much had happened during her absence which required both her presence and her acknowledgment. One of the prices of stardom was selflessness. An actress should be alive and breathing only on stage and a puppet of her audience off. Or so it seemed to Ivy as her mother and Colin swarmed around her.

"I'm sorry," Colin said. "But you'll have to get dressed. Drury Brent has invited us to a small gathering at his place. Since you weren't available, I accepted for you. By proxy."

Colin spoke as though she had committed, not a crime of indecency, but a crime of neglect by going out for so long without calling him.

"Thank you for covering up," she said, meaning it.

She glanced out between the chintz curtains and saw a haze of indigo drawing night across the sky. Only coincidence had brought her home in time to prepare for Drury Brent's approval. And she certainly couldn't afford to overlook an invitation from one of New York's most influential critics.

"I'll be ready in a minute."

Her family had a way of disappearing whenever Colin arrived. Even her mother became half invisible, speaking softly, controlling her natural mannerisms. She felt glad that no one would dare pounce on her for the moment. It was easier to hide behind glamour than argue with parents who didn't particularly respect her.

Without further comment, Ivy went to her bedroom. Only by accident had she escaped a tremendous blunder in strategy. What if she had stayed out another few hours and missed her social debut? What if Colin had decided to be suspicious of her absence? She had come dangerously close to pressing her luck past the breaking point.

She took out a simple white gown which flattered her fine proportions by covering instead of revealing them. The high, Chinese-style neckline molded her breasts and revealed the graceful arch of her neck. She did her hair sleekly, fastening an emerald spray into the coil of braids crowning the top of her head. Only a woman who didn't care would keep jewels about as carelessly as she did. The pose of nonchalance suited her and intrigued Colin. Living with the family worked amazingly to her advantage. It made her unique in Colin's experience. She knew it irked him that she wasn't so easily available as he might wish. Any other girl in her position would be glad to take an apartment of her own so Colin could do as he pleased.

Ivy inspected the finished product of herself glittering regally in contrast with the middle-class surroundings of clumsy bed and dressing table. Arched eyebrows, fine bridged nose and wide, compelling mouth protected the harried little girl inside and must always protect her. She draped a scarlet cape of silk along her back and lay the ends into the crook of her elbows. The languid scent of *Flamme Diable* gave a final touch of urgency. She had achieved the effect of desire floating about her as though without her awareness. Her eyelids lowered for a second in recognition of the irony. Then Ivy swept out of the bedroom, chin high, eyes glowing.

Colin took her downstairs to where his limousine stood double parked. The chauffeur opened the door with respectful elegance and Ivy arranged herself in full comfort before Colin got in beside her.

"Is anything the matter?" Colin said as the automobile eased through traffic. "You seem … I don't know. Remote."

She looked into his questioning face and patted his hand reassuringly. But how could she reassure Colin when she couldn't comfort herself? Of course she was remote. She had run off and hid somewhere because life was neither real nor earnest. Because her body was a cardboard figurine that could topple over at any moment and blow away to the arms of a man who could only reject her.

"I'm sorry," Colin put in quickly. "You're entitled to the temperament of your profession."

She knew that Colin was making excuses for that mysterious part of her which hovered beyond his grasp. For his sake, she was glad that he did not know the real truth of her problem. But how long would he accept his own excuses? How long before he started to question why the woman who was supposed to love him did not confide in him completely?

"You'll enjoy yourself tonight," he added, as though he needed an excuse for barging in on her privacy.

"Drury's a weird bird. And nobody's fool."

"I don't doubt that," Ivy said with a chuckle. She had often read his brutal columns with admiration. Any man in Drury Brent's position could be devastating. But his judgments were the result of a penetrating fairness. He had no use for sham and sniffed it out with the uncanny nose of a bloodhound. But when he came upon a real talent, he spared no effort to help it reach the peak of success. She felt curious to meet him and flattered that he desired to meet her.

They stopped in front of the private house Drury had purchased and remodeled. Its black filigree gate clearly defined the end of public domain for idle curiosity seekers.

Passers-by stared after Ivy as she swept up the circular staircase, her stole shimmering like a flame in the growing darkness.

A small intelligent-looking Oriental bowed Ivy and Colin inside. Pieces of sculpture done in wood and in stone seemed to lead the way into a larger room where several people were already comfortably seated. Ivy knew all the faces. Old timers of the theater who had proven themselves and who had lasted through fads and depressions, like vintage wine. A little thrill scintillated in Ivy's veins. She felt that touch of humility which had happened before only in Mike's arms.

"Colin. Glad you could make it."

The man who approached seemed to be walking on hot coals. All of his square bulk moved rapidly and with decision. A bulky hearing aid stopped up his left ear and its cord looped down into the handkerchief pocket of his black satin jacket. Drury was not one for new fangled gadgets when an old dependable one had proved itself worthy.

He stopped and looked with a second's graveness at Ivy. She felt all the doors of her secrets become transparent in the single moment of piercing recognition. Drury's eyes were a catlike yellow, flecked with black and brown and orange. His shiny brown hair was soft and short. She could imagine it standing straight up on end when he became angry. And she was positive that Drury's anger was something she never wanted to experience.

"Hello, Ivy Sherwood," he said. "You know, we are going to become very good friends."

The way he said it made Ivy believe every word. And she felt herself being swathed in a great kindness. The sort of kindness which cradled her, dissolving all problems as though her personal life were but a childish nightmare.

Before she had a chance to reciprocate his graciousness, Drury began introducing her to the others.

Perhaps she had expected to meet gods. But the stellar names proved to belong to people whose conflicts and problems had taken their toll, leaving the scars of battle on their faces.

Shepard Duncan, a matinee idol twenty years ago and now a great tragic actor, greeted her too ceremoniously to be sober. Ivy watched him try to blink her into focus, the romantic eyes very blank and wavering. Occasionally he was known to go away for short periods. Only his closest friends ever knew whether he had taken off for a binge or a sanitarium.

The woman beside him took Ivy's hand and clasped it warmly. "You gave me great pleasure, last evening." Her voice was a little too deep, her hair shorn a little too abruptly for true womanliness. Yet on stage. Astrid Pettit was the epitome of everything feminine. Housewives copied the hair styles of her wigs, not realizing they were wigs.

And so Ivy met them all, each betraying a human frailty so well disguised behind make-up and footlights. The difference in this gathering from any other was a fine wrapping of dignity which encased them all, like cellophane. The dignity of art, worked for, sacrificed for and worshipped as a sacred river that meanders through arid country.

Only Colin did not seem part of it. He hopped, skipped and jumped above the waves of misfortune, simple in heart, profound in health and secure in pocket. She had never really observed

Colin in this way before. He fixed a double Scotch for himself and brought her a liqueur.

"I hope you've had dinner," he said.

She noted an undertone which asked more than the simple question about food. It asked for her to volunteer what she had been doing all afternoon.

"I stopped by an ice cream parlor." She took the glass and sipped from it.

Colin grinned. His large, easy-going face relaxed once again into confidence.

She turned away from his naive trust and joined the conversation between Astrid Pettit and Drury. He was telling her something about a log cabin in Connecticut.

As Ivy approached, he got up from his chair so she could take it. But he did not interrupt what he was saying or glance at her. It was an instinctive action that made Ivy feel like a piece of his property which he was accustomed to taking care of. It made her curious to know more about Drury Brent. And what he wanted from her.

Astrid said, "I don't think I'll come visit you up there, Drury. Made an ass of myself last August with some little brunette." She twisted a cigarette into a short ivory holder. "And the repercussions are still drifting down to me." Her voice was neither sad nor apologetic. Amusement flicked over her lips and twinkled in her almond shaped eyes. "Have you made an ass of yourself recently, Ivy?"

"All the time," Ivy said. The unexpected ring of truth in her own manner startled her but neither of the other two.

"Good," Drury said, taking notice of her now. "Don't look surprised, my little one." He set her glass on the marble topped table.

Drury was laughing at her silently, Ivy knew. Was it fashionable to be foolish?

"Spontaneous release is a fine antidote for sophistication," he concluded.

Ivy tried to seem at ease in the presence of these apparently careless attitudes toward living. She put her arms along the curving slender arms of the Queen Anne chair and waited for Drury to go on.

His yellow eyes became sharper. "You'll come to visit me, won't you, Ivy. Or do you, too, have skeletons in Connecticut?"

She met his gaze directly. One could not flinch and be friends with Drury Brent at the same time. "I'd be delighted to see your cabin."

"Fine. Next Saturday."

The suddenness of his invitation did not surprise her. And Drury's manner of phrasing requests in the form of a gentle command pleased her. His confidence reminded her of Mike, in a way.

As she thought about Mike, Drury Brent became suddenly very important to her. She had the feeling he could teach her strength and self-control.

But any feelings of self-possession inspired by Drury Brent deserted Ivy by the time Colin took her home again.

"You don't have to come all the way upstairs," she said, nuzzling him on the cheek as they stood in the shadows of the staircase.

"All right, darling. See you tomorrow. Sleep well."

She waited for the sound of his automobile to mingle with the traffic before she went out again.

The cold night wind chilled her beneath the thin material of her dress. Her delicate stole gave no protection as it flapped and clung to her. Vaguely, she felt herself shivering. But she had to get to a telephone. She had to speak to Mike, if only for a second, and straighten this thing out about Hilda. She knew it didn't make sense to pester him. But none of her made sense. The thought of that woman lying in Mike's arms, enjoying his kisses, inflamed by the touch of his mouth on her body.... Hatred and anger screamed inside her, whipped by humiliation and need.

The saving thought of Drury had long since slipped away beyond her grasp. He floated in the back of her mind like a distant, tiny bubble.

She found a cigar store and closed herself into the narrow phone booth. Hurriedly, she dialed his number and listened to the phone ring impersonally and methodically.

At last she heard his voice.

"I've got to talk to you," she said. Her voice was strained and pitched too high.

He didn't want her to come down again tonight. He gave her a dozen intelligent reasons why she should stop being seen so often in his cheap neighborhood.

But they made no difference.

She hailed a cab and sat tensely in a corner, huddled in the knot of her own anxiety and impatience.

When she burst in on Mike, he was still sitting on the divan as though he hadn't moved all day. But he must have moved because the room looked cleaner somehow, dusted and tidied. Ivy pressed her lips together tightly, forcing herself not to curse Hilda aloud.

"What is it this time?" Mike said. He took a pipe out of his back pocket and began to tamp down the loose ends of tobacco.

Alone with him now, all the words fled. She knew only desire. She took the pipe out of his hands and placed his fingers on her breasts.

"Only that I love you." Her voice was rough.

"Do you?"

He tried to sound casual, but she could feel the rise of his own passion. She knew Mike better than he knew himself. They might destroy each other but they could not hide behind false words.

Ivy's stole dropped to the floor. Her own hands searched the line of muscles on his chest. "Don't push me away. Please. Don't make me beg for you."

An instant passed in which they both sat rigidly. Then, like a burst of lightning through black sky, he grabbed her. They fell off the divan together and rolled on the carpet. His fingers caught her collar and ripped it down past her satin brassiere. She helped him tear her dress the rest of the way, not caring about how she would get home later. Gladly she would have torn off her skin if this were the way to keep Mike. The day's frustration, the month of craving for him surged in great waves and burst against Mike. Her teeth bit into his lips and she arched herself against him, straining every fiber of her being to unite with the man she loved.

"Oh, hold me...keep me," she cried, half in prayer, half in savagery.

Her knees slid along his narrow hips. She felt his fingers pulling the roots of her hair and her braids fell away to swing wildly about as she twisted with Mike in a still closer embrace. Her elbow banged on the floor and bruised unheeded. She felt his tongue on her throat and rose toward it.

"Love me...love me always." The words were breathy, muttered.

It maddened her beyond endurance that he didn't speak. That he wouldn't commit himself to promises she could remember. But he was real and she held him in her arms. For a moment she could believe this would go on forever. Mounting passion made her trust that Mike would not force her back into the outside world after the moment passed. She lay groaning and smothering beneath his weight, possessing him with every muscle in her body that could clamp tight and hold its beloved. The fire in him flared and fed the searing flame of her own body as they moved together toward oblivion and surcease.

She felt she would crack wide open and spill across the earth. Then with a sudden tremendous leap, her back arched tight as a bow. It curved up harder, higher. Higher.

A small whimpering sound escaped from her lips, mingling ecstasy and sadness.

After awhile the world began to return to focus. They lay apart, breathing rapidly still, but calming surely, inevitably. Ivy stretched out a hand and laid it tenderly against his cheek.

"All right," he said. "You've got what you came for. You can go home now."

The words knifed through her. But his attitude was not new. She always had to steel herself for this moment. Each time it was a little worse. A trifle nastier. A trifle more aloof. How could he be so distant now, when they had just been as close as two human beings can achieve?

"Try to be kind," Ivy whispered. "Just once in awhile." She groped about for his pipe, slipped it between his lips and brought a flaring match to the bowl.

"Is that what you want, kindness?" He puffed out clouds of smoke that curled toward her soft naked breasts. "I doubt it. I doubt it very much."

Ivy had used up all her arguments many times before. She was not about to lecture him that even blind men had a place in the scheme of living. She knew that Mike's refusal to do something productive was not a matter of cowardice. Only those who knew Mike as well as she did could understand the greater courage it took for him not to compromise. That any work he might undertake must be an intolerable second best. All his life he had dreamed about architecture, studied it and then practiced the profession brilliantly and successfully. To do anything else for him was no better than sitting on a corner with a tin cup.

"Mike," she said, ignoring his bid for an argument, "Why are the pictures off the wall?"

He turned to her, as though his eyes could see and inspect her face. "I gave them away," he said evenly. "Are you looking shocked, my dear?"

"Frankly, yes."

He took the pipe and pressed its mouthpiece to his forehead. "I gave them to an admirer."

"You what?" She sat up into a flood of soft lamplight. Then she realized that the lights had been on when she came in. "That woman has been here all day and all evening, hasn't she? And you gave your pictures to her, didn't you?"

"Why must you use that accusing voice, Ivy? What is your magnificent pride going to do for you?" He reached about on the floor for his pants, found the cuff and pulled them to him.

His words stung her with their truth. "And your pride? What about that?" No matter what he did, she could not accept the fact that Mike had given up his battle. She clung, deep inside her, to the firm knowledge that secretly he was still figuring out a plan to bring him back to work. An impossible idea, but Mike was that kind of impossible person.

"Let's not rehash the business of my pride," he said, standing up and fastening the dungarees. "It bores me." He took careful steps across the room and felt the hands of a glassless clock.

"All right," she said. "Throw me out, if that's easier than answering a simple question."

"Everything's so simple to you. So clear. So black and white. Yes, go home. I want you to go home. You drive me nuts with all this do-gooding. That's one thing I can say for Hilda. She takes me for what I am. Now go on. Get out."

Slowly, Ivy put her clothes back on, draping the stole over her shoulders and tying it to hide the ripped bodice of her gown. A small glow of satisfaction began to buoy her up. As long as Mike could feel guilty about Hilda, he didn't really want her. The thought was like a straw floating on the ocean. But somehow it felt strong enough to carry Ivy to shore.

"I'm coming back tomorrow," she whispered as she kissed him. "And I'm going to get back those pictures."

# CHAPTER FOUR

IVY LET herself into the house and tiptoed past the sound of her father's snoring. By the time she got into bed, it was after four o'clock. Her body felt all used up. The lassitude of fulfillment made a pleasant ebbing sensation in her limbs. Her plans for Mike became dimmer and finally wandered away into sleep.

But her dreams shattered abruptly.

She fought against waking. She tried to cling to the fairy tales spun by her subconscious world. The harsh knocking on her door grew louder, more insistent.

"All right," she mumbled. "I'm up. Go away." She pulled the blanket over her ears in a vain effort to gain a last few minutes of sleep.

The door opened. A hand shook her shoulder. Her eyes squinted open, fighting against the streamers of daylight. She saw her father's eyes. They fixed on her with that peculiar gleam of icy blueness which meant he was determined not to be put off.

"Sit up, Ivy." He stood at the foot of the bed, jangling keys in his pants pocket. "You're never home at night so I can talk to you. You think by running around like a crazy one you can avoid me?" A wisp of fading hair stood up on his balding head like a cock's comb.

Her head felt soggy from sleep. She sat up and fixed the pillow behind her. A dull throbbing started inside her cheek bones. Blearily, she leaned over to her wrist watch. A quarter of seven. He had an hour to rant at her before he had to go off to work. She settled back and waited.

"I don't know what you're doing with yourself lately. But I can guess." He pulled out the chair from her dressing table and sat down, close to the bed. "You think I'm stupid, maybe. Or maybe you think you're all grown up. Well, let me tell you this, young lady." He stabbed the air with a forefinger. "I'm laying down the law to you right now. I want you home every night by one o'clock. And when you don't come home, I want you to pick up the phone and say where you are. All this selfish carrying on. You're driving your mother crazy, worrying what could happen to you."

Ivy sucked in her breath, trying to control the anger and the resentment. If he really cared about her, she would have known it, felt it long ago. By now she understood that her father had given her up as a lost cause. He didn't really care what she did, so long as it was covered with the pretense of respect for him.

"Do you hear me?"

She gazed at a fleck of tissue stuck to a shaving nick on the side of his chin. He was acting very powerful, very much the ruler in his own home. But underneath the bluster, she knew he was as weak and as lost as herself.

"I hear you," she said.

"All right, then." The fight petered out of him because she hadn't argued. "Behave."

She waited for him to leave. But he didn't seem to know how to get up and walk out. He licked his lip, unsatisfied by the too-easy conquest.

"Look at you," he spluttered. "You look half dead."

But the conversation was finished. She allowed him to splutter out a few last words to balance the energetic prologue.

When he finally left her in peace, she slid back under the covers, knowing that she would have to move out of the house. It was the only way to prevent bitterness from filling up the rift which had grown so wide between herself and the family.

A feeling of isolation surrounded her. She wished she could go back to sleep and stave off the loneliness for another hour.

Instead, she went to the bathroom and ran hot water into the tub. Carefully, she lowered herself and began to rub soap on the worn wash cloth. It was funny how years ago she used to think that reaching stardom would solve all her troubles. She thought about Mike and about Colin and about her family. Her troubles were only beginning.

She drew the cloth between her toes and eyed the gold polish on the nails. The sandals she wore in the second act required this odd color. She surveyed her feet, remarking how soft and unspoiled they looked. Mike used to enjoy stroking her instep. Once he had made a plaster model of them, using each for a book end. But the sculpture had long since disappeared from his apartment. Just as the pictures had gone.

Yes, the pictures. She had made up her mind to seek out Hilda and get them back. Buy them if necessary. Her lazy motions became more rapid as she calculated that there was time to do so this morning and get back for Colin to drive her to the theater. She lathered circles around her breasts and into the hollows of her arm pits. She stood up and let the water drain out of the tub, then crouched beneath the faucet and rinsed herself off.

When she came out of the bathroom, she heard Leo slamming the refrigerator door. He was at the stage where eating consisted of grabbing nibbles. The thought of Leo warmed her. He would grow up and go to college and be something his father could take pride in.

She took a pair of camel hair slacks from a hanger and pulled a green bulky knit sweater over her head. Then she wiggled her feet into a pair of ballet slippers and combed her hair simply but neatly.

When she came into the kitchen, Leo stood leaning against the sink, his cheeks stuffed with pie. He held a glass of milk in one hand and was wiping the other on a dish towel.

"You up so early?" He spoke around the stuffing in his mouth. "Where's Mom?"

Leo shrugged. "She's got some kinda pain in her back. Still sleeping, I guess."

"Who made Dad's breakfast?"

"Musta' made his own."

A twang of guilt plucked at her. She didn't want to see the family's disintegration. She put some water to boil for instant coffee, needing the lift of caffeine. Leo fastened an old leather strap around his books while she spooned the powdered coffee into a dime store mug.

"I gotta run," he said.

She watched him take off, envying his high spirits, wondering how long it would be before Leo, too, saw and understood the age creeping up on his folks.

She drank the coffee black, enjoying its scalding bitterness. The phone began to jangle out in the foyer. She hurried to it, wanting to catch the sound before it wakened her mother.

Colin's first response, like Leo's was to ask what she was doing up so early.

"Is there a rule against it?" she answered impatiently.

No, there was no rule. He simply thought she'd been looking tired lately and needed more rest.

This repetitious concern about her health irritated Ivy's guilt. "Well, since I am up, you can tell me what you want and get it over with." She had no right to jump on Colin but she was in a mood to jump on anyone.

He had only wanted to say that he'd be by a few hours early so they could have lunch together and have a few words with her press agent.

"I don't need any words."

But she did and she knew it. Only she didn't have the patience to postpone her trip to Hilda.

Evenly, Colin tried to convince her that she wasn't in a position yet to be so nonchalant about her publicity.

"Then how about after the matinee?"

Colin paused. When he spoke again, he sounded as though he were dealing with a child who had to be cajoled into taking its medicine.

His tone sickened Ivy because she realized she deserved this attitude. And then it occurred to her that Colin was bound to get suspicious if she continued to act in a way which seemed unreasonable to him. And suspicion was one thing he must not feel. It could lead him to discovering her relationship with Mike. Then only Heaven knew what mayhem would take place.

"All right, Colin," she said. "I wasn't thinking."

She let the receiver drop into its cradle and walked back and around the kitchen like a caged thing. After three more cups of coffee, she felt steadier. She went to her mother's bedroom and peered in.

"What are you doing up so soon?" Evidently she had been awake and listening all this while.

Ivy felt spied upon. "Is it so strange? Wherever I turn somebody asks me the same question." She came in and sat down on the edge of the bumpy mattress.

"Yes, it's strange." She pushed aside her long hair, revealing the pallid complexion usually hidden beneath generous amounts of rouge. "For you it's strange, anyway. Don't tell me you got up all by yourself." She tugged at the neckline of her flannel nightgown.

Ivy folded her hands between her spread thighs. "Well, if you must know, Dad woke me. He decided it was time to come forth with a nice, fatherly lecture."

"Maybe you deserved it?" Painfully she shifted her position and smoothed the quilt around her thick waist.

"So I deserved it. But he makes me feel like a two year old. And I'm not going to stay around and listen to him sound off like that."

"If you didn't act like a two year old, he wouldn't treat you that way. You think he likes to yell at you? A grown girl? A daughter who should be a comfort to him?"

She knew her mother didn't mean to claw at her open wounds. But she also knew the futility of expecting anything different.

"I don't know what to say, Mom. Except that maybe I'd better move out of here before it gets worse."

"Running away? I tell you, don't make it worse and it won't get worse. I know how it is to be in the theater with all kinds of people who have no morals. They influence you. But it's just not right for a young, unmarried girl to move out of her home."

"You mean you wouldn't know how to explain it to the neighbors?" Ivy felt compelled to hit back.

"I wouldn't know how to explain it to myself." Her breaths came out with effort.

"It's very simple," Ivy said, struggling to regain her sense of kindness. "He's the boss in this house and that's how it should be. But he's not my boss anymore. He doesn't give me an allowance and he doesn't walk me to school or pay for my clothes. And he's in no position to tell me how to live or run my career." She said the words without hope that her mother would agree. But they had to be spoken. Her reasons for leaving had to be out in the open and subject to whatever prejudiced examination they might receive.

"You're talking nonsense," her mother sighed.

"All right. I'm talking nonsense. But it isn't nonsense to me. And I'm getting my own place, approval or no approval. Now please, let's not have any further argument."

Beneath the conviction, Ivy felt like a child running away from home in the middle of the night. She couldn't understand why it worked out that way. Her beliefs seemed to speed ahead of her like a ball bouncing downhill. She could not catch up with her feelings and make them appear to others the way they seemed to her. But regardless of what her mother thought, she knew she was going to leave. That she must leave. That, for better or worse, she had a right to her own way of life.

"Should I boil you some eggs?" Ivy asked. "Leo told me you weren't feeling well."

"I'm feeling fine," her mother said and reached out for the woolen bathrobe lying at the foot of the bed. "But you want to boil me an egg? So boil me an egg."

Ivy went back to the kitchen, knowing there was nothing she could do that would take her over the barriers of misunderstanding. Listlessly, she ran water into a dented aluminum pot and adjusted the flame of the gas stove. She set pieces of silver carefully on the checked linoleum table cloth and brought out a plate of sliced rye bread.

She wondered what Drury would think of her now, if he could see her creeping about this house, defeated and whimpering. A broad grin suddenly dispelled her gloom. She knew what he would think. And what he would say. She could imagine reading it in his review: THE SHERWOOD FAMILY, A TIRED MELODRAMA IN THREE ACTS. TOO TIRED, IN FACT, FOR ME TO MENTION FURTHER.

Her moment of self-pity scampered away.

By the time Colin arrived, she had changed to a navy wool suit that gave her body an air of reserve set off by the ladylike charm of a cream colored blouse.

The dark circles under her eyes were expertly covered by her skill with make-up. She looked fresh and alert and young and when she spoke, she made her voice lilt to carry off the act completely.

She watched Colin beam as he looked at her. His thoughts rode across his forehead like the lettered light bulbs that brought out the news around the *Times* building. He was proud of this possession he had discovered in a Greenwich Village theater. Pleased with himself for nurturing it. Superior for not letting it slip away from him now it had reached maturity.

"Shall we be off?" he said after a brief greeting to her mother, who tightened the cord of her bathrobe self-consciously.

Ivy got her purse and smoothed on a pair of navy gloves to make him wait for another moment. She felt a perverse desire to torture him. To make him a trifle insecure beneath the nice white shirt and expensive tweed jacket. Perhaps someday she would have the freedom to tell Colin the truth about himself. That she had no more taste for his maleness than for a dried crust of bread. That she had never belonged to him any more than the dozens of others who came and went from her life.

He cupped his hand on her waist and steered her out the door as though she couldn't find it for herself. She wanted to dig her heels into his shins. But she smiled and pretended to listen to his chatter. The golden words which would tarnish in an eye wink if it weren't for the fat checkbook.

In the car Colin brought out a package of her brand of cigarettes and handed them over. She took them, feeling a surge of shame for the hatred that consumed her. If there was hating to be done, she was not the one who should do it. But even as she peered through this keyhole of justice, Ivy could not bring herself to feel any friendship toward this man. Her world was colored and bruised by Mike. She was indeed poison Ivy. Poisoned by her need for him. By her lack of him. If only the blue marks on her thighs were the only scars...

"I wanted to save it as a surprise," Colin's voice broke in on her thoughts. "But now I'm not so convinced that you're going to welcome it."

"Welcome what?" A rush of air came through the slightly open window and made the cigarette smoke invisible.

"The news Ed Denny has for you."

"Stop playing with me, Colin, please. I have a headache."

He leaned across her and rolled the window up. "Ed got you a spot on the *Star Fire* show. Just a five minute or so interview between their song and dance routines. But it's a break for you, my dear. Give all America the chance to see you. In person."

Her crossness dissolved. A chance on the *Star Fire* show was not easily come by. No publicity could compete with this. "Oh, Colin, I don't appreciate you. I really don't."

She moved closer to him so that he could kiss her.

"You could start appreciating," he said low in his throat. "You could marry me."

There it was again. The cold, hurtful challenge to her privacy. Whenever Colin spoke about marriage, she wanted to run from him. Or yell that she could never belong to anyone except Mike. But she was locked in the car with him. And she owed Colin a great debt. She must try to be more affectionate. At least human.

Carefully she inched out of his grasp and patted her hair. She took out a pearl compact and removed the top of her lipstick. Obviously, she couldn't speak if she were fixing the color on her lips. And she needed the few minutes to think of something to say that she hadn't already told him a dozen times.

"I wish I could understand you," Colin filled in the silence for her. "It's been almost a year already." He mashed out his cigarette in the small gleaming tray and snapped the lid closed.

"There's nothing to understand," she answered lamely. "I suppose I'm just too wound up to think clearly."

The limousine slowed in the convergence of mid-morning traffic. Taxis bleated and jammed closer. Her head felt as clogged and noisy as the day outside. She asked the chauffeur to close his window too.

"What is there to think about?" Colin persisted. "You have all the advantages, you know." He spoke matter-of-factly without any hint of pompousness.

All the advantages except one, Ivy thought.

There was no use denying that Mike was holding her back. Not only in her personal life, but in her career as well. If it weren't for Mike, she would be steadier and more aware. But her constant need of him was like a perpetual hangover that pained and made her tender.

"We'll drop it," Colin said briskly.

She was glad he had the faculty to preserve his pride.

The limousine pulled up on a side street off Broadway. She went with Colin into the famous restaurant where everybody who was anybody in theatrical circles gathered to eat, joke and do business.

The large room was crowded and noisy and waiters carried trays high above their heads. Colin wended a path for her between the tables and over to a reserved circular booth. He pulled out the table and she slid inside, pulling off her gloves finger by finger. She tasted ice water from a huge goblet and surveyed the thousands of photographs, signed and smiling, which hung in thin black frames. The clatter and conversation bore down on her but she managed to preserve the unique aloofness which was her trade mark.

"Ed's always late," Colin said. "Would you like a Manhattan?" As he spoke, he nodded hello to various people at a distance.

Ivy felt grateful that he had not stopped to introduce her to them. She felt that she had just so many smiles left in her reservoir and that she'd better dole them out carefully.

The waiter brought Manhattans and set them on green cardboard coasters. She lifted her glass and sipped because Colin expected it of her. She wanted to be as conventional as possible according to the code of stars and their satellites. And as she surveyed the crowd, she noticed that most of them were straining to do the same thing. She saw a short ivory cigarette holder bob between elbows.

"Is that Astrid Pettit?" she said.

"Where? Oh yes. Funny, but she doesn't usually come here this time of day."

Ivy felt curious. "Why not?"

"I don't know. She just doesn't."

She didn't want to voice a desire to speak with Astrid now. Perhaps after they finished business with Ed Denny, if there were still time.

He finally came in, scowling, his shirt open at the collar, looking not at all like the conventional press agent. But he was the best in the business or Colin wouldn't have hired him.

Ed reached the table and straddled a spare chair. He took a plastic cigar holder out of his pocket and jammed it between his thick lips without the cigar. Bearlike fur curled out from beneath the cuffs of his shirt as he reached across the table and brought Colin's Manhattan to his mouth. Ivy had never seen anyone capable of drinking with a cigar holder. She liked the man because he hadn't tried to learn New York polish.

"Okay, little girl," he said, putting down the emptied glass and tugging a folder paper from inside his jacket. "Put your initials right there so I can get out of this lousy place."

She had expected some kind of conversation from Ed. A how-are-you. Something.

"Well? Colin told you, didn't he?"

"He didn't tell me everything."

Ed groaned. "Oh, for Chrissake. What do you want to know? Some old bag got the gleeps and dropped out. So I grabbed the spot for you. What else? Next Sunday night. You can make it. Don't give me any of this razzle about other engagements."

Ivy smiled. He was worth one of her smiles. She took the pen Colin had placed on the tablecloth and put her name on the paper. "Thank you, Ed."

"Yeah. You're welcome." He pushed the chair out from beneath his meaty legs and shoved the paper back inside his pocket. "I might even watch the show," he said, unable, for the moment, to resist Ivy's smile.

He made his way like a steam roller back through the crowd.

"That's my boy," Colin said.

She watched Ed stop and lean over at Astrid's table. He said a few words between his clenched teeth and then continued toward the door. A few moments later, she saw Astrid stand up. She seemed a trifle more feminine today because of earrings that blended in with her hair-do. She was dressed in shades of pale and forest green which brought out auburn highlights. Astrid glanced around, evidently looking for someone. Their gazes met and Ivy raised her hand just enough to wave slightly

Without further invitation, Astrid began moving toward their table.

Colin said, "I wonder what's got into her?" He was speaking more to himself than to Ivy.

"Hello again," Astrid said. "I didn't expect Colin to bring you into this menagerie."

"I don't very often. And what the heck are you doing here, anyway?"

Tiny wrinkles of laughter formed around the edges of her eyes. "Window shopping," she said casually. "Simply window shopping."

"I don't believe you. But let's get you a drink for service beyond the call of duty."

She tapped her cigarette holder on the back of Colin's hand. "Dear, take some advice from an old-timer. Don't try to make quips. From you, they fall heavier than yesterday's doughnuts."

Ivy struggled to suppress laughter. She had never been quite able to pin down what made Colin such a drag. Astrid had summed it up beautifully. She touched the seat beside her. Astrid sat down there.

"I'm glad we ran into each other again." She accepted one of Ivy's cigarettes. "Colin has a way of hiding his precious possessions in a miserly way which does not endear him to his friends."

"That's not true," Colin objected.

"Of course it isn't, dear. I was only fooling." She relaxed back in the semicircle out of Colin's view. "How does it feel to be you, Ivy? Now that the shouting's begun."

"Still nervous," Ivy admitted. She had no intention of pulling any of the phoney temperament that fooled Colin.

"You'll learn to get used to it. Live with it like a mother-in-law." She balanced the holder against the ash tray. "But if you'd like some company, you might try one of our famous hen-gatherings where all the girls wail unashamed and go home feeling much relieved."

She had timed her sentence for the moment when Colin was preoccupied with speaking to the waiter.

"I'd like that."

"Yes..."

"Like what?" Colin interrupted.

"Woman talk, do you mind?" Astrid's open expression attested to her innocence. "But if you must know, I was comparing notes about the theater. Brings back my own youth."

"I'll bet," Colin said with a slight edge to his voice.

Ivy could have slapped his face. She had no female friends whatsoever. It would do her good to have the company of a woman with whom she could let her hair down.

Ivy finished her drink more out of anger than because she wanted it.

"I'd better be getting back to my own table," Astrid said. "Besides, it's almost curtain time."

When she was out of ear shot, Ivy turned on Colin. "I thought you people were friends," she said hotly.

"We are." He lifted the menu and studied it. "But Astrid is, shall we say, more of a buddy."

Ivy knew what Colin meant. A wave of resentment pursed her lips. She had seldom seen the meanness in him. And now it loomed gigantic. But she made herself eat a sandwich, all the while not talking to him. She promised herself to give Colin twice as hard a time as he had given Astrid.

They strolled to the stage entrance of her theater.

"See you about five," he said.

"Don't bother." Her words were clipped. "I want to walk home by myself."

She whirled and stalked inside, leaving him to stare after her in consternation.

The performance went well. In a way, Ivy felt it a relief to become someone else for a few hours. It gave her own conflicts a chance to seek for a solution without the reigning influence of her conscious control. She sat in the small dressing room blotting the top layer of smeary stuff off her face. Then she smoothed on a thick layer of cold cream while the costume woman hung up her things and took out her street clothes.

A few bouquets had arrived, but certainly not as many as on opening night. She glanced methodically over the cards, recognizing none of the names. She was looking for some token from Mike. Any little something would thrill her. But he wasn't the type for Valentine cards or birthday presents even in the days of their closest intimacy. The honesty in Mike revolted against formal pre-arranged recognitions. Whenever he had bought a flower, it had arrived unexpected, and not because she had grown a mechanical year older, but in response to the mystic urge of love which had occasionally overwhelmed him. She sighed with nostalgia and went behind the screen where her stockings and underthings lay on top of a trunk. As she fastened the stockings, she let her hands linger on the marks he had made last night. Her elbow was black and blue where she had hit it. Right now, she could run right down to him and let him bruise her body all over again.

Ivy fastened her skirt and waited, knowing she could not yet go out on the street unless she dressed better or hurried into a car. In ten more minutes, the theater would be empty and then she'd be free to go out, walk along Broadway or go someplace for the few hours left to her before the evening performance got under way.

But if she stayed here, Colin would come to fetch her. And she could not stand to see him now. Given the legitimate reason of his manner toward Astrid, she could free the energy of all her other reasons not to see him.

She decided to risk the crowds by going out ahead of time.

It was quiet enough in the alley. But the moment she reached the sidewalk, someone screeched, "There she is!"

It was a sedate noise compared with the way movie actresses were treated. But this was Ivy's first experience with an unrestricted audience. She saw programs being jabbed at her chest. She took the extended pencil and scribbled her name. Another. Yet another. She stood there writing, without seeing where she wrote. Drowning in the mill and push. Smiling nodding, intoning thank-you's, while she saw only the dizzy whirl of pressing faces and more pencils.

Miraculously, a large uniformed bulk shouldered its way through the crowd and led Ivy away with an authority she could not protest against. He brought her to the door of a gleaming maroon Rolls.

Astrid leaned out, took her hand, and pulled Ivy inside. "I saw you getting the works out there," Astrid said sympathetically. "You looked like a little blonde shepherd being eaten alive by his own sheep."

Ivy slumped back and felt the perspiration beginning to stand out on her flesh. She rested her closed eyelids in the palm of her hand while the car pulled away toward Eighth Avenue.

"Now there," Astrid draped a lap rug over Ivy's knees. "You aren't old Aunt Minnie, after all."

"I'm sorry." She straightened up and accepted a hard candy from Astrid's purseful of supplies.

"Don't be sorry. Just be cleverer next time. Why did you come out all by yourself like that anyway?"

"To tell you the truth, I wanted to avoid Colin."

"Oh?"

The moment she'd said it, Ivy knew it was a mistake. She could not follow through with the rest of the truth, nor would she tell Astrid a lie. "Please don't ask me to explain," she said.

Astrid took the candy wrapper from Ivy's grip and stuffed it into the elastic pouch attached to the front seat. "I don't have to," she said.

Ivy felt her earlobes begin to redden.

"Oh, don't be embarrassed for my sake. Colin wasn't talking through his hat, you know."

She looked squarely at Astrid and found only melting consideration in her eyes. They were a hazel color, now blue, now green, depending upon her mood and surroundings. "Nevertheless, it was uncalled for."

"Well, thank you for your spirited defense, my child."

She saw that Astrid was more than accustomed to having things said behind her back. Not only was she accustomed, but she seemed to expect them. It made Ivy wonder. "Colin said he didn't often see you in that restaurant."

"True enough. But I'm sure you wouldn't fight with him because of that."

"Were you there today... for any particular reason?"

Astrid rocked her head back and laughed silently. "Oh, my dear little Ivy. Colin doesn't think I planned to be there on the chance of meeting you?" The laughter became audible now in rollicking waves that dismissed Colin as an imbecile not worth considering.

"I don't know what he thinks," Ivy answered gravely, "but I don't want to be anywhere near him."

"You needn't be, I'm sure."

"I wish I were so sure."

"Would you like to come up to my place and talk it over?"

Ivy realized how Colin would fume if he ever found out. But nothing he could say or do would make her beware of Astrid. She had never met a person who combined humanity and humor in such generous proportions.

# CHAPTER FIVE

Astrid's apartment housed two maids, three fox terriers and a parrot sitting on a horizontal bar.

She made no comment about her pets. Ivy understood that the reasons for them were self-evident. To each person his own expression of loneliness and fear about the encroaching dark that moved steadily closer beyond one's control.

The rooms themselves comprised a spacious suite in one of the more fashionable hotels overlooking Central Park on the East Side. The furniture was simple and comfortable without either Drury's ornateness or Colin's flash. Astrid herself dominated the decor, moving with limpid yet strong motions that fascinated play viewers and friends alike.

"A glass of hot cocoa would be good," she said to Ivy. "Especially for one who doesn't have to watch her figure yet." She could have been speaking about herself, though she meant Ivy.

"Yes. Fine. You have a lovely place here."

"I inherited it when my sister got married. Been in the family since the building first went up." She patted amber cushions into one corner of a long sofa and reclined against them.

"I'll have to be getting a place soon," Ivy confided. "Family growing pains."

"It's a common story. Been hunting around?"

One of the maids brought a silver tray and set it on the square coffee table. Whole wheat toast in diagonals stood in a holder. Ivy took a piece and bit into the end of it.

"Not yet. I made the final decision only this morning."

They chatted about apartments available around New York and gradually Ivy's tension resolved itself into the happy prospect of having Astrid's help in finding a suitable place.

The few hours till curtain time flew by.

When Astrid dropped her at the theater, Ivy felt calmer and more confident of herself. She realized how much she had missed by not having any real friends during all the years she'd been working for stardom.

Colin was pacing her dressing room when she came in after the last act.

"You worry me," he said, blowing smoke through his nostrils. "I have the sneaking suspicion you're going to hell with yourself."

Ivy flounced across the small distance to the screen. "Can you wait outside till I'm dressed?" She had no intention of getting embroiled with Colin. An argument might lead to searing truths which neither would be able to forget. And she needed Colin still.

"Yes, I'll wait outside. But it wouldn't surprise me if you left through the window."

She caught his hurt tone and softened a little. How could she expect Colin to understand things he didn't even know about? And Colin had no reason to think that she had never really loved him. She was a better actress than he knew.

"I'll be with you in five minutes," she said, ignoring his thrust. "Promise."

He turned the door knob and left.

She put her clothes on slowly, in no rush to go to Colin's apartment tonight. But this was not the time to feign excuses. He needed to be soothed and made to feel secure again in her affection. For all his bluster and hobnobbing, Colin had a shaky and sensitive pride which he tended carefully. If he discovered that she was making a fool out of him, he could not take it philosophically. Colin's revenge would be mean and destructive. She sensed that beneath all his willingness to do things for her. She felt it beneath his patience and trust.

When Ivy came out of the dressing room, she managed to be all smiles and coziness. She linked her arm through his and kept her body very close to his hip.

He put his palm over her wrist, obviously placated. "I meant it, Ivy," he said. "You do worry me." But now he sounded less worried.

"To tell you the truth," she said, "I am a little jumpy."

She told him about the autograph hounds and how Astrid had rescued her. She was prepared for him to be nasty about Astrid, but she preferred that he hear the story from her own lips. That way he would be convinced that the afternoon was innocent.

"I can get you an apartment faster than anyone else. You know that."

They were standing on the corner of Broadway, waiting for Colin's automobile. The blinking neons reflected pink and blue on his face. She saw that he was anticipating the pleasures and conveniences that would be his once she moved away from home. And since she had made it sound as if she were making the move for his sake, he really could not be offended that she had spent the afternoon with Astrid.

She despised him for feeling so triumphant. She despised herself for the half lies, half truths which ruined any hope of personal integrity.

But she had regained Colin's confidence. "Would you like to take me home?" she said. "I'd get a real lift out of starting to pack."

Her request sounded logical. And it implied a compliment to him.

"But first, let's have a cup of coffee someplace," she added to strengthen her advantage.

"Of course," he agreed with sympathy that came from renewed power.

They rode downtown to a basement espresso place and settled themselves at a tiny round table in the shadows. She had often come here during the lean years of poetry reading for a dollar an hour and bit parts in plays that folded after two nights. Some of the waiters recognized her and congratulated her with sincere pleasure. But none of them stayed very long to chat, sensing Colin's protective coolness. He guarded her with a hungry intentness that revealed to Ivy the full, vast depths of his insecurity. She realized he never spoke about his own family. And he'd never introduced her to his friends other than the theatrical cronies with which he surrounded himself. Suddenly he became for her a starved hobo wandering on the rim of other people's lives.

But her feeling of compassion for this man had limits which became even narrower as she compared him with Mike. Her nerves began to tighten as she thought of him. If Colin weren't here, she could walk the short distance to his house. And she had told him she would come. She could spend the night fighting with him, making love. Anything. It would all be precious because it was shared with Mike.

She tasted the cappuccino and added sugar to the strong cinnamon flavor. Already her mind was planning to sneak back down town after Colin took her home.

Her expectation built a haze which screened out Colin's conversation. She faintly heard the tone of his voice and managed to nod during its pauses until he finally paid the check and brought her home.

As soon as he was gone, she hurried around the corner to her own car and raced down town to Mike, her mind suddenly clear, her senses sharp. All the night sounds and soot smells of the city touched her. The cold, smooth wheel felt good in her grasp. She seemed to have come awake from a long hibernation.

Mike was sitting at the kitchen table, his hands working with a large mound of plasticine.

"Ivy?"

"Of course. Am I interrupting you?"

"Would you go away if I said yes?"

"No."

"Then sit down and be quiet."

She sat for a half hour, watching Mike's touch bring a horse's head into being. His fingers seemed to search in the amorphous mass until they found the head and saved it from eternal burial.

Mike tilted his chair back. "How does he look?"

"Powerful." She contemplated the flaring nostrils and the tossing mane. "He looks ready to fight with another stallion for the love of a young mare."

"You're disgustingly romantic," he chuckled.

She felt grateful that Mike was in a good mood for once. It had been a long time since she had found him doing something constructive.

"You know what you can do?" he said, picking the clay out from around his cuticles.

"What?"

"Take us for a ride to Coney Island. I'd like to hear the sound of the waves before winter sets in." His tone had mellowed and his large eyes stared diagonally downward, seeing, not the dirty molding, but a vast expanse of ocean.

"All right," she answered softly. "I'd love to."

He reached in her direction and touched her jacket sleeve. "Are you dressed for it?"

"I'll be fine."

"No. You'll be cold. Get my navy sweater for yourself."

She was glad to do anything he asked.

From the closet, she got the sweater and brought down the large woolen blanket they used to take on picnics. Flutters of delight drifted down on her like confetti. Could she dare to hope that Mike was coming out of his dark well of despair? She dropped her jacket in the living room and pulled his heavy sweater over her blouse, rolling up the too long cuffs. Then she bundled the blanket under her arm and returned to the kitchen.

She appraised his denim shirt. "What about you? Don't you want to wear something over that?"

"I'll be fine," he said with conviction.

He followed her down the steps, holding the bannister lightly, his canvas shoes making a soft, spongy sound on the worn slate.

In the car she dropped the blanket on his lap and nosed into the flow of traffic heading toward the Brooklyn Battery Tunnel. She lit a cigarette and put it between his lips. Happiness swelled almost unbearably in her heart, choking off the need for conversation.

Soon the tang of salt air touched her nostrils. Then the great loops of the roller coaster appeared against the sky, huge and silent. She drove along the deserted avenue and through the ghost town of gaiety, feeling in her spirit all the animation necessary to bring Luna Park alive.

A few youngsters were buying hot dogs at Nathan's. They waved and whistled as the white Lincoln passed by.

"Your fan club," Mike said.

"Don't be silly," she said. "They don't know me."

"Maybe not yet." He folded his arms. "But soon enough, my dear. Soon enough."

She grunted uncomfortably, not wanting to think about anything except Mike. After passing a few blocks, she steered the car into a side street that connected with the boardwalk and parked near the wooden steps leading up to it.

Mike rolled the blanket under one arm and got out of the car. He stood with one hand touching the edge of the door until she came around to him. He took her arm.

She remembered when they used to walk, how he would always be a step or two ahead of her, his long strides making her work to keep up with him. Now he was the barest fraction of an inch behind her and she tried not to feel that she was leading him.

They came up on the boardwalk and into a swift wind that tousled her hair and flung it about her shoulders. She felt Mike's chest expand as he breathed in deeply, the limp collar of his shirt flapping madly but unnoticed as he leaned toward the water. They found a bench and he spread the blanket over her and put his naked arm behind her neck. His skin felt warm and vibrant.

She gazed past the blowing sand to white crests slamming down on the cold shore. The boardwalk lamps were very dim, unable to lighten the distant surging blackness. All the litter cans had been taken off the beach until next summer and behind them, the custard stands and games were boarded up. Only an occasional policeman could be seen leaning on the rail or swinging his night stick in an effort to maintain life in this bleak solitude.

Ivy snuggled closer into the hollow of Mike's arm, partly from cold, partly from her desire to get inside of him, share his breath and his blood.

"I've been needing this," he said after awhile. "It's hell, cooped up in that stinking apartment."

Ivy lifted her face into the wet air and touched the salt vapor on her lips. "We could rent a place on the water, if you'd like."

"We? How is Miss Four-Stars going to explain it to her slavering audience? And besides," he continued more sensibly, "It would be damned inconvenient for you to travel into the city every day."

"I could manage. Lots of people commute from Connecticut."

"Out of the question."

Yet his dismissal refused to discourage her. "Tell you what," she began.

"Don't tell me anything. Let's go down to the water."

He folded the blanket and tossed it over his shoulder while she bent over and took off her heels.

In stockinged feet she plunged through the icy sand. Drops of water were flung across her cheeks by the high wind. The throaty ocean yawned dangerously close as though ready to suck them into a curving wave.

She wasn't leading Mike now, but following him. He walked as though he could see it all, his profile tipped upward, his forehead wrinkled with the intensity of a seventh sense. He stopped just short of the water's edge and continued to walk along the edge of the surf, following the pungent odor of moss and rotting wood pilings till they reached the dank shelter of a pier.

Beer cans and yellowed newspapers lay half covered by cast off tires and sand.

Mike bent down and gradually spread the blanket, feeling and discarding trash as his hands reached them. Then he lay down on the blanket and clasped his hands behind his head.

Ivy needed no invitation to join him.

She put her face on his chest and slowly undid the top button of his shirt.

Mike sighed and began to massage her back in small circles which moved gradually down along her spine. She felt his palm cup her buttocks and continue till it met the curve of her thigh.

"We could live on the beach, Mike," she said, half dreaming. "Build a house of driftwood, go surf fishing."

He laughed and turned so that the wide belt dug into her. "Sure. You'd make the ideal beachcomber."

But with Mike lying warm underneath her, it didn't sound silly. She let her hand slide to his waist. She could live anywhere, in a garbage truck if necessary, so long as Mike were with her, like this. Her hips eased themselves between his thighs, dragging her tight skirt up past her knees. The sound of water flowing and sliding away gave a rhythm to her own movements.

His hands probed up beneath the sweater, yanked the blouse free and undid the hooks of her brassiere. Then they slid around to the front of her and squeezed her nipples, urging them into shivering points.

The tight skirt restricted any real freedom of her legs, annoying her with an inhibition she did not want. Impatiently she pulled it way up till it circled her hips. The sudden feel of cold air on her almost naked behind made her shiver in a sudden convulsion. But this did not stop her. She worked impatiently to free herself from the girdle.

The strong beam of a flashlight hunted out and found her nakedness.

Ivy whirled to face the inquisitive policeman.

"That's enough of that," he said. "Come on, get out of there."

Ivy knew two things and both horrified her. Either she could go docilely to the police station and accept the repercussions on her career or she could plead her way free by using the sympathy angle of Mike's blindness. She began to straighten her skirt, her mind refusing to make a choice.

"Officer," Mike said. "Come over here a minute, will you?"

"Take it easy, buddy."

"I seem to have lost my bearings. Will you give me a hand?"

Ivy stopped, paralyzed by the humiliation Mike was about to undergo for her sake. She watched him grope for the cop's searchlight and shine it directly into his eyes.

"I'm not kidding you," Mike said.

The officer took a long, uncertain breath. Then he snapped off the light in a self-conscious action covered up by bruskness.

"I don't ever want to find you here again," he said. Then he turned in the damp sand and strode away, anxious to escape his own embarrassment.

Silently Mike got up and folded the blanket. Then he took Ivy's arm and they went back to the car.

All the way into Manhattan, she tried to find something to say to him. Puny words of appreciation were useless. All of her trembled hard as she fought to prevent the tears from overflowing.

When they reached his apartment, she flung herself into his arms. Sobs wrenched out of her and the burning tears soaked into his shirt. He cradled her till she calmed.

"I'm sorry," she said. There was nothing else to say.

"Don't be," Mike answered evenly. "It wasn't your fault."

"Then let me stay with you tonight," she pleaded.

Nothing could make her leave him now.

They went into the bedroom, undressed and lay beneath the neat covers. She watched him lying on his back, rigidly in possession of a deep hopelessness. She prayed he would move to touch her, but she did not dare make the first overture herself. Only God knew what terrors Mike was controlling.

And she was still watching him and hoping when the first rays of morning slivered through the window.

The sound of Hilda shuffling in to fix breakfast made Ivy's teeth clench. She wanted to go in there and squash her into the wall. She wanted to annihilate everything that resulted from Mike's incapacity.

She got out of bed, put on her slip and strode barefoot into the kitchen.

Hilda's eyelids drooped, but she said nothing. Her scrawny hands clawed strips of bacon from the package and dropped them into a pan.

"We won't need you anymore," Ivy said slow and cold. "If you'll tell me what Mr. Devlin owes you, I'll be glad to pay."

"Hmmph. The slut talks like she's got a marriage license. I don't see no wedding ring, dearie."

In one blinding action, Ivy's hand slapped the bony face. The pan came off the stove and crashed against her shoulder bone.

Mike appeared in the doorway. "Stop it. Both of you. Stop it!"

The two women slunk silently away from each other, confronted by his towering fury. His hands gripped either side of the door frame, the knuckles white. He looked like a blind Samson who could destroy the world in one sweep.

"All right, Hilda," he said in a more controlled voice. "You can go now."

She crept past him without looking back.

When she had closed the door, he said, "And you can go now, too."

"Mike, please."

"I said you can go."

There was no arguing with him.

She touched the horse's head and tried to remember that his moment of happiness last night had really existed. But whether it had existed or not, it had been effectively swept away. If she hadn't come, the beach episode wouldn't have occurred. A tremor of remorse shook her. It was her fault. It was. It was!

But she dressed obediently, moved by the dull knowledge that she was no good for Mike. The less she indulged herself by coming here, the better off he would be. Without her, he might find his own way to some accomplishment. With her, he was forced beyond reason to a show of masculine protectiveness.

For Mike's sake, she must stay away from him. The seething desire in the pit of her stomach must not be allowed to destroy the one thing she loved.

Once she had thought that Mike was the unreasonable one. Maybe he had been. But now everything was too complicated and she could find no place to put the blame. Whosever fault it was made no difference. All that mattered was that Mike must be allowed to find himself.

And this he could only do if she walked out of his life once and for all.

When her clothes were in order, Ivy stood on her toes and kissed him lingeringly on the cheek.

Then, like Hilda, she crept out and closed the door. But unlike Hilda, she would not be back tomorrow. With all her might, she wished she could turn into the straggly witch who was privileged to serve Mike Devlin.

She wandered aimlessly through the grey city and stared at the people in their fresh morning clothes as they got aboard buses and hurried into train stations. To make a life for herself without Mike. To make a life for herself that meant something, that could give pleasure to others .... This was to be her greatest role. Her life must become one long inspiring play until the curtain dropped finally and the audience went away forever.

Her years of theater training made Ivy acutely sensitive to drama. She could see the threads of Mike's life intermingling elsewhere, untouched by her own. Yet he would always carry within himself their times of being together and this memory would touch everything he did.

She stopped into a busy drug store and ordered coffee, trying to shake herself free from desolation. The time had come for her to begin thinking in terms of substitutes for her love. Sublimation, the books called it. What use could she be, walking the earth like a mourner, blind to the favor destiny had bestowed on her career? She would be indeed blinder than Mike not to recognize that his faith in her was based on reality. For if he did not believe in her, why had he sacrificed himself last night? Wasn't it his way of saying that her career was more important than even their intimacy? Yes, Mike's faith lay in talent, its development and use. He despised people who possessed God's gifts and flung them away for selfish lusts.

She must not let him down.

The coffee stirred her a little. She surveyed her reflection in a mirror beside the line of telephone booths and realized she was a shambles. Two runners went up her stocking and her skirt was all accordion creases. She looked as if she'd been doing exactly what she had been doing. It was no compliment either to herself or to Mike for it to show this way. She paused, wondering where she might go to fix herself up before she had to see Colin or anyone else who was in a position to ask questions.

Once again, Ivy had to face the fact that she had no close friends. Astrid might help her, though. And she certainly wasn't the type to pry. She couldn't afford it.

Livening somewhat, she took a cab to the hotel and strode imperiously by the doorman as though she were draped in chinchilla.

But it wasn't Astrid who greeted her when the maid opened the door.

Shepard Duncan teetered across the room with Astrid's parrot sitting blandly on his shoulder. He held his fine large head aslant, trying to remember where he had seen Ivy.

"Hello, Mr. Duncan," she said, almost glad that he was in no condition to notice her condition. "I'm Ivy Sherwood. We met at ..."

"Yes, yes." He lifted the bird off his shoulder and offered it to Ivy. "I do remember you. Thank you for coming to see me."

She wondered if he realized he was not in his own home. The parrot had wrapped its claws around her jacket sleeve. She stood watching it blink, not knowing quite what to do.

"And please don't call me Mr. Duncan. It makes me feel cold."

Ivy carried the parrot to its stand and pushed him onto the wooden bar. "Is Astrid here?"

"Oh," he waved his hand through the air. "She must be someplace about. She always is." He wandered off toward the bedroom, circled around and came back. "We'd better wait for the lady's entrance."

Ivy did the best she could to make herself comfortable on the sofa. She assumed that Shepard was drunk, but he seemed to have a functioning shrewdness which belied his condition. If he were only pretending to be drunk, she wondered why it was necessary.

Shepard touched his one dark eyebrow with his middle finger, then ran the finger across his temple and through the pure white hair. "Do you know what I am doing? I am waiting for a telegram."

She tried to discover what kind of reaction he wanted from her.

"The time will come when you, too, my little one, will wait for telegrams. We all do. Astrid waits. Drury waits. Oh, you won't get them to admit it. But they wait."

"A telegram from San Diego, California, where my wife is vacationing with our lovely children."

"How nice," she said helplessly.

"No. It isn't nice at all. In fact it's goddamned lousy."

Ivy remembered reading that Shepard Duncan had been divorced for twenty years and never remarried. She decided it was better to keep quiet and let him do the talking.

She couldn't imagine Drury Brent waiting for anything. Bits of sand scratched inside her bra. She needed to shuck off her clothes and submit to a hot cleansing shower. Wash Mike off her, out of her. Shepard's conversation was not helping to raise her morale. She felt what he was talking about more than he realized.

"I'm depressing you," he said with quick perception. "Well, remember the emotion. It will come in handy one day on stage."

Mercifully Astrid came in now from the bedroom. She wore lemon yellow pajamas, tailored severely, but so soft that they molded her firm breasts provocatively.

"Oh my," she said. "What's all this going on?" She did not seem surprised by Ivy's presence.

Ivy suddenly felt a sense of belonging which did more to raise her spirits than an hour long spilling of confidences. No one had ever taken her for granted without wanting to tie a leash around her neck.

"I need a bath," Ivy said directly. "And to borrow some clothes, if they fit me."

"Apparently," Astrid said. "Come along before Shepard makes you miserable."

He thumbed his nose at her in a spurt of disarming boyishness.

Ivy followed her into a large bedroom done in shades of blue. Two photographs stood in a silver frame on the dresser. Both of the same person. Ivy recognized the face. It belonged to a French actress who had died last winter in her ninety-seventh year.

Astrid noted the direction of Ivy's thoughts. "Yes, she was marvelous." There was no regret in her voice. Nor sorrow. "Everything brilliant, noble and demanding." Astrid's voice spoke like a person who had tasted the best in life and was glad for the experience, rather than grieved at its finish.

"I've been thinking about an apartment for you," she continued. "There's a place off Madison Avenue that I like. If you hurry, we might run take a look."

"What about Shepard?" She unbuttoned her blouse and hung it on the back of Astrid's reading chair.

"Well, what about him?"

"I mean, we're going to leave him all by himself?"

"Oh, Shepard's always by himself. Was he giving you the story about waiting for a telegram?"

"Yes," Ivy answered, disappointed.

Astrid laughed and stretched her arms in the sheaves of sunlight. She looked like a stalk of wheat swaying in a field. "You should have been warned. It's his way of saying, welcome to the Happiness Club."

Ivy had all her things off now. She stood naked and waiting like a little girl.

Astrid turned. Her sharp eyes darted over the bluish bruises, then focused directly on Ivy's face. "That way," she said and pointed to a half-open door. "Take whatever you need while I hunt you up something to wear."

Ivy paddled into the bathroom and shut herself in behind the glass door of the shower. She turned the faucets and a needle spray raced down on her. In Astrid's presence, it was terribly difficult to feel sorry for herself or anyone else, for that matter. A good influence, Ivy decided. Definitely a good influence.

She did a quick job of cleaning herself, alert to a new freedom that made her feel light and joyous inside. There would be no time in her life to think about Mike. The nasty urge which plagued her would simply have to go away and bother somebody else.

Yet even as she thought this, Ivy knew she was being too eager. The solution wasn't so simple as she wanted to believe. There were many long nights ahead to be faced alone. Nights when desire bit into her as though with pointed teeth. Nights when she would not be able to stand the four silent walls pressing in on her.

But she sang to herself as she washed. Then she patted and rubbed a deep Turkish towel over her skin, making her blood race healthily. She wrapped the towel around her and tied it between her breasts, then stepped back into the bedroom, tracking wet footprints.

"Ready," Ivy said.

Astrid came away from her wall length closet and dropped some skirts on the bed. "Try these. One of them ought to fit."

As Ivy tried the different sizes, she realized that the skirts certainly could not all belong to Astrid. But she wouldn't allow her mind to dwell on what they were doing here or to whom they did belong.

One of them, a black cashmere, fitted well enough for Ivy to wear on the street. Astrid's stockings and camel hair coat, together with her own blouse, completed the job.

"You'll do fine," Astrid said, meanwhile pulling on a one piece knit dress which accentuated the compact femininity of her hips. She was an exceedingly attractive woman of the debonaire school. Only those who saw her at complete ease could spot the quality about her which was different from normal women.

Normal? Ivy had no concept of what was supposed to be normal. During the past few months, her ideals and judgments had been turned upside down and shaken out. Looking inside herself for answers was like taking the back off a watch and trying to discover what made the hands go round. Impossible for the untrained eye. For more than twenty years, she had been fortunate enough to take herself and the way she ticked for granted. Now that she had to inspect and make choices, an army of difficulties chased down on her. She would have preferred to stand still and let the decisions happen. But her preference was of no account in the business of living from day to day. For all her good intentions, the part of her that needed Mike moved restlessly.

"You don't have to primp," Astrid interrupted her complex of feelings.

"All right, then. I'm ready."

They both returned to the living room where Shepard had fallen asleep on the couch.

"He comes here every few months," Astrid said. "Whenever the magazine scribes want to do an article. Says it gives him courage to be interviewed with Treasure Joe," she nodded at the parrot.

Astrid left a few final instructions with the maid and then they went quietly out. Ivy still found it difficult to believe that the business with the telegram had not been real.

The apartment off Madison Avenue consisted of four large rooms in which their footsteps resounded on the bare floor. A usable fireplace centered in the living room and in the bedroom. The kitchen had a small alcove for a dinette set and the rooms were high enough up from the street to muffle the sounds of traffic.

There was no reason on earth why Ivy shouldn't lease it. But she had a premonition of loneliness which made her hesitate. She searched Astrid's smiling eyes for assurance and then agreed to sign a lease before the thing that haunted her won out.

Hastily she started to make talk about furnishings, needing to mingle herself midst the reality of rugs and cabinets.

Astrid had all the answers. She had apparently been quite intimate with an interior decorator recently and she overflowed with advice and addresses of off-trail stores.

They stopped into Astrid's favorite place for lunch before show time. Ivy ate and ate, convincing herself that she needed other sustenance than Mike's touch.

She had wanted to become mature and independent, she had wanted to act the role befitting a young star. Now was the time to do these things. Now was the time to bend her frustrations into creative endeavor.

Suddenly she reached across the table and squeezed Astrid's hand. "Do you really think I can become a good actress?" she asked, imploring, beneath the words, for sustenance to carry her along.

Astrid smiled with understanding. It reminded Ivy of Shepard's talk about telegrams.

"You'll be a wonderful actress," Astrid said, squeezing Ivy's hand in return. "One needs only to work ... and not think."

# CHAPTER SIX

IVY PLUNGED into her new life of independence with the fury of desperation.

Between shows, she hurried to all the decorating stores and buried herself in the whirlwind of making purchases. She ordered carpets, oil paintings, wall paper, without plan or logic, drowning herself in the acquisition of objects with the fierce compulsion of a drug addict. But at night, she could not sleep on her new bed. She lay on the foam rubber mattress, surrounded by the screaming, aching vastness of her need for Mike. Occasionally she would fall into a fitful nightmare. Dreams of obscene pleasures would rise from her subconscious and she would fight to wake herself from them. Bathed in a clammy sweat, she wandered around the strange apartment, pushing a Chinese cabinet from one wall to the other, hanging and re-hanging pictures, shifting table lamps and tables. Anything to stave off going back to sleep again. Anything to prevent yielding herself to the sharpening teeth of terror. Her life was becoming a ferris wheel that circled madly around the clock, ever faster and faster.

For two days, she managed to see little of Colin, using the excuse that she needed to get settled in the new place. Actually she could not face him. She sensed that if he tried to touch her, or kiss her, she would beat her fists into his face and mash him to a pulp. Her nerves quivered on the high pitch of exhaustion.

But Thursday evening, he refused to be put off any longer. After the evening show, his grip tightened on her arm and he led her forcibly into his car.

Ivy sat very still and stared out the window, sending pulsa-
tions of anger along the sides of her face. All her good intentions
to be sensible about Colin had long since vanished. She knew
only that he meant to keep her prisoner for his own lust. She
hated him actively, blindly, without logic.

"You're working too hard," Colin said. He did not try to put
his arm around her, but settled for touching her knee lightly.
"You've taken on too much for one person, darling." He laughed
in what sounded to Ivy like an idiot's cackle. "I mean for you to
rest tonight. Forget your responsibilities for a few hours. Do you
good."

She didn't answer him. She had no intention of speaking to
him at all.

He steered her into the elevator and then into his apartment
and sat her on the deep cushions of a large chair. "Now, I don't
want you to move," he said. "I'll fix us a couple of drinks and
we'll let the rest of the world go by."

Stonily she remained in the chair. Colin brought over two
highballs, sat down on the arm of the chair, leaned over and
touched his lips to the side of her neck.

"Now, isn't this better?" he whispered against her hair.

The misery she'd been fleeing seemed to catch up with her all
at once. There was no escape from Colin, none from herself. She
tasted the whiskey and wondered if people like Shepard Duncan
could really find escape by drinking. She rolled the stuff around
on her tongue and swallowed.

Colin was talking to her but Ivy did her best not to listen. She
tasted some more of the alcohol. Her empty stomach seemed to
reach up and claw around it. Then the sensation passed and she
began to feel a bit more comfortable in the chair. She wiggled
her feet out of her shoes. She began to think about the world of
routine and intelligence and moderation and to wonder if such
things really existed. She continued drinking in little sips while
she thought. The room was really very quiet. Pleasanter than the

noisy streets far away. Much pleasanter. And she began not to mind so much, Colin's closeness.

She jerked her head away when he nipped at her. Then she thought: the devil with it.

Yes, the room was really pleasant. Her skin began to feel warmer. She sensed the rhythm of her pulse slackening. She smiled without knowing at what she smiled.

After a while, she held out her glass to him. It was empty.

"Another?" Colin said.

"Uh hmm." She extended one foot and surveyed the toes glittering goldly through her stocking. They amused her. She remembered *Kismet* and Marlene Deitrich's gold-painted legs. How lovely to be an actress. How delightfully unreal.

Colin slid off the chair and poured more whiskey over fresh ice cubes. He put the glass into her hand and she brought it to her lips automatically.

She began to feel like a balloon with the air going out of it slowly, evenly. Peaceably. She giggled at a private joke without knowing what the joke was.

"Well, now," Colin said, taking away her emptied glass. "I didn't know you were so thirsty."

"Who's thirsty?" she said. Her voice sounded a long way off.

A window shade banged in one of the other rooms. She heard the sound through a wall of rubber beginning to rise spongily about her. She felt strangely protected from all harshness. A touch of confidence was beginning to make her cheeks rosier. She squinted a little to keep the room in focus. But it was too much trouble. Everything was too much trouble. She shrugged her shoulders and all the troubles lay down and rolled over like trained dogs. And all the little dogs had Mike's face.

"I'll take another," she said.

Colin hesitated. "There's no rush," he said with feigned mildness.

But Ivy quaffed the third drink with growing zest. The whiskey sloshed inside her, filling all the corners of her viscera. With sudden clarity, she knew what her goal was.

She wanted to drink herself insensible. Anesthetize herself so that Colin would possess, not Ivy Sherwood, but a limp, useless vessel. The alcohol would freeze her brain, blur Mike's image, destroy the lunatic passion raging in her heart.

The muscles inside her thighs tightened. Wispy fingers began to crawl along the curve of her hips. She pushed herself out of the chair and poured more alcohol into the tall glass, filling it almost full. She tilted her head far back and snapped the burning liquid down her throat.

"What are you doing?" Colin demanded. He reached her in two fast steps and grabbed the glass away. "You must be losing your senses."

Ivy rocked back on her heels and stretched out her arms to a vision of Mike which seemed to be dancing just beyond her fingertips' reach.

"Oh, how I love you," she breathed. The words came out slowly and a trifle thick.

"You show it in a very unique way," Colin said, twisting the stopper back into the bottle.

She didn't hear Colin's voice. She heard only Mike, breathing and living inside her. For a week she had tried to flee the terror of needing him. But now, she wasn't frightened at all.

The room began to rock slightly under her feet. She could smell the whiskey fumes on her own breath. She giggled as the joints of her body began to melt and she buckled slowly toward the floor.

"Ivy! For heaven's sake, get up from there." Colin knelt and tried to raise her.

Ivy draped her arms around his neck. "Tell me you want me, darling, tell me ... tell me." Her eyelids fluttered closed. Their edges crinkled in a little smile.

"Of course I want you. But you must stand up." He braced his biceps beneath her armpits. He dragged her to the sofa.

She fell back heavily, pulling him with her. Colin tried to untangle her arms from around his neck. "Don't go away," she said. "Not yet. Not before we..." In a quick jabbing action, she thrust her lips against his. Her mouth opened and she began to squirm and wriggled her body for contact with the heavy, massive maleness so close.

Her flaring skirt gave plenty of freedom. Her knees parted. Her fingers twisted into the collar of his jacket. Snakelike, her legs went around his body and held him to her. She could not understand why her clothes were still on. A pouting annoyance niggled in her hazed mind. She let go of Mike with one hand and started to tear her clothes away, moaning insensibly, wriggling frantically, harried with the urgent need for their bodies to really meet.

She could tell that for some unknown reason, he wasn't pleased. He felt tense and awkward. But she could conquer that. She began fumbling with his clothes too. Her fingers were weak as spider legs, nimble yet somehow ineffective.

"Undress me," she pleaded.

She felt him beginning to yield. His fingers searched out and found the zipper of her dress.

In a few moments, she was lying almost naked on the sofa, her brassiere askew on one shoulder, her stockings sagging below her knees. With both hands, she lifted her breasts until they touched answering flesh.

"Oh, take me. Take me."

A piercing sensation consumed her. An electric whirr shivered along her spine. She strained upward. She bit and clawed and perspired. Mike seemed to come down on her with the weight of a thirty foot placard.

She gurgled and groaned in soaring ecstasy.

The pounding crest of completion roared in her ears. It flung her onto the shore and left her lying there, exhausted. She turned on her side and snuggled her cheek beneath his chin.

Gradually her eyes opened. She kissed the line of his jaw. Puzzlement creased her forehead. It wasn't Mike's jaw. She sprang up and stared into Colin's face.

Ivy felt herself go white. All the blood in her body seemed to rush to her diaphragm. Nausea rose violently. She heard a wretched scream without realizing that it was her own voice.

Colin gripped her wrists. He began to shake her. He picked her up, kicking and screaming, and carried her into the bedroom. She fought against the tablet he tried to work between her lips. But for all the anguish, she was too weak. She swallowed the tablet and sipped a little water.

In a few moments she began to feel a cloudy sensation of detachment. The horror seemed to belong not to herself, but to another. She could sit back and view it. Then a spell of grogginess made her bored with the horror. She didn't want to contemplate it any more. She let herself slip into a lying position. How delicious it felt not to have worries.

A heavy drugged sleep claimed her.

Ivy awakened with a terrible thirst that swelled in her mouth and almost choked off her breath. She got out of bed, rushed to the bathroom and put her lips beneath the faucet. She drank deeply, seemingly without end.

Panting, she straightened up to the reflection of swollen eyelids peering at her from the square mirror. She had to work to remember what day it was. Friday? Saturday? She wasn't quite sure. But as she conjectured about this, the desire for water returned. She filled the plastic drinking cup and swallowed, still watching herself over its rim.

Painfully, mercilessly, she began to recall what had happened. She closed the door carefully and locked it, needing to protect herself from Colin till she understood the full meaning of her experience.

There could be no doubt about the success of their union. The familiar, placid sensation blunted her nervousness. She recognized her lassitude and could not possibly attribute it to the sleeping pill. After all these years of fighting, she had managed at last to free herself from the jail of her frigidity. But by no means could she consider it a healthy freedom. She had achieved success through bringing to bear such a vivid hallucination of Mike's presence that the mere recollection of it made her tremble. Perhaps this was the first step toward the brink of madness.

Quickly she brushed away this thought as being ridiculous. Melodrama again. Any actress worth her salt could imagine things more vividly and react to them more vividly than other people. Especially under the influence of alcohol, considering the fact that she was not accustomed to drinking. It was the combination of too much whiskey on an empty stomach after a week of fitful sleeping that had done the trick. It had accomplished the thing she'd been striving for for so long.

She ran the cold water again and patted it on her burning cheeks, drinking some from her cupped hands. Then she stood watching the water swirl down the drain. Could she dare to hope that last night's success might be repeated?

She heard Colin's footsteps approach the door. He knocked gently. "Ivy?"

"I'm all right," she said. Her voice was weak but clear. "How much time do I have before curtain?"

"About two hours."

"I'll be out in a moment." She considered the show and realized that it was the one stabilizing force in her life. Regardless of how far from reality she might soar, there would always be matinee and evening to draw her back to earth.

She unlocked the door and went out for her clothes.

Colin was waiting for her in the living room, his face pale but controlled. "Maybe you oughtn't go to Connecticut tomorrow," he suggested mildly.

Drury Brent! She had forgotten all about him. The country was just what she needed right now. Take her away from Colin … and from herself. Drury's presence would fill her with a good dose of sanity. Her face brightened.

"Of course I ought to go," she said with enthusiasm.

"Are you sure?" He was looking at her as though she were made out of china.

She turned away from this judgment of her capabilities without answering him.

"I mean …" He searched for the right words. "Well, after all, Ivy. What am I supposed to think?"

"Whatever you wish." Her sharpness ended Colin's objections.

She wanted to ask him what she had said last night. But if she betrayed herself about Mike, Colin would have mentioned something.

No doubt, he merely thought she had been drinking too much in general. Good. Let him believe this. Hide the truth.

But Colin came to her and grabbed both her elbows. "Now you listen to me," he said. "I've put up with enough of your nonsense. Whatever you've been doing is no damned good and I want you to stop."

"Stop what, Colin?" She felt elusive, evasive. He could not really reach her any more than she could reach Mike. They were like two smoky ghosts facing each other in the middle of nowhere.

He let go of her suddenly. "I see there's no use trying to talk sense."

"No, there's no use," she echoed. Poor Colin, little did he know how replaceable he was by anything that wore trousers.

"I didn't know you were an alcoholic," he said bitterly.

"You should've had me screened." The words twisted bitterly from her lips.

With a sudden jab it occurred to her that she could very possibly become an alcoholic. Now. She thought about finding Shepard Duncan and going on a month long bender with him. They would make great buddies.

Colin sighed helplessly. "If you'd only share with me what's troubling you." His arms hung listlessly in mid-air. He looked like a wind-up toy that had suddenly run down.

"Believe me." She straightened the seams of her stockings. "There's nothing."

She meant this sincerely. If her life depended on it, she could not find meaning in the complexities of her impulses. She felt in the midst of some medieval curse which would forever evade the cold light of scientific analysis.

The most she could do was seek here and there for temporary relief. The companionship of people like Astrid and Drury, who could accept her without trying to make healthy the sick part.

"All right," he said. "Let's get some breakfast."

Until after the matinee show, Ivy kept the lid tightly shut over her curiosity. Whenever it popped up, she told herself that last night had been a freak, most probably. She musn't count on it to happen again. Really, she should forget about it altogether.

When the curtain fell, giving her a few hours of freedom, she hurried the three blocks across town to Astrid's theater. She did not want to be alone.

Astrid came stalking out from the stage door, collar turned up to her chin, hands jammed into her coat pockets, her normally pleasant manner coarsened and steely. She spotted Ivy, managed to smile, took her elbow and steered her into the Rolls.

"I hate leading men," Astrid said from tight lips. She took one of Ivy's cigarettes and puffed voluminous smoke clouds, not bothering now about the feminine prop of her ivory holder. "Snotty little bastard." She was speaking to herself.

Ivy knew about actors' arguments. They were the worst kind. Tempers raged and tore with the vehemence of life itself. She sat without talking until Astrid cleared the anger from her system.

"But why am I taking it out on you, poor thing?" Astrid smiled suddenly. "I'm really glad you came to get me. How's the apartment doing?" Though she was trying to be sociable, the scowl had not completely left her voice.

"So so," Ivy said. She did not elaborate. Neither of them really cared very much about such trivia.

"Good."

Ivy wished she could distract her friend. She felt a little worried by the masculinity which had broken through to the surface. It made her feel a trifle unsteady to have the real, unadorned Astrid, the bare guts of Astrid before her.

They reached the hotel and Astrid flung herself into a chair without bothering to take off her coat. She sat for a moment and then she jumped up again and began to pace the floor. One of the terriers gamboled around her feet. She bent down, scratched his ear absently, then pushed him away.

"You want to talk about it?" Ivy said. She folded herself unobtrusively into one corner of the sofa.

"What's to talk about?" Astrid laughed grimly. She ran her fingers through her hair. "I hate men, that's all. I hate every goddam prick that walks."

"You don't hate Shepard," Ivy said in a little voice. "Or Drury."

This observation quieted Astrid. "No. Of course not." She plumped herself onto the other end of the sofa. "Don't mind my fits. They're harmless."

Ivy felt somewhat relaxed. But still, it wasn't the same Astrid. They were not like two women sharing a tete-a-tete about the problem of men. She did not know what, exactly, to make of this vibrating presence with fierce eyes and deepened voice.

"I could do with some gin," Astrid said. "Will you fix it for me, honey?"

A tiny thrill passed across the edge of her upper lip. "Of course."

Ivy searched out the gin behind the many bottles in the cabinet. She ran her fingernail around the seal, conjecturing whether all alcohol had the same effect on a person.

"If you press that wall button, you'll find an ice box with some quinine water in it."

Ivy pressed the button. She enjoyed being told what to do. It took the responsibility away.

She gave Astrid one glass and settled down beside her, holding the other glass tightly between both hands.

"How's Colin?"

The question seemed strangely out of place, somehow. Ivy brought her feet up and tucked them under her thighs. "I guess he's all right." She raised the glass to her lips now so she wouldn't have to talk anymore about him.

"Is that how it is?" Astrid said. Beneath the words ran a current of understanding. She drew her arms out of the coat, revealing a shirt of soft blue wool.

Ivy wondered suddenly how old Astrid might be. Her extreme boyishness sliced away the years. She watched Astrid stretch her feet across the cushions and cross them at the ankles. They were lovely ankles, slim and sleek.

But though her mind was full of moving thoughts, Ivy could find no conversation. She was glad that the drink did not taste like alcohol. This gave her confidence. No doubt, she could drink half a dozen of these mild things and nothing would happen. She shook her head and the masses of blonde hair fell over the sofa's rounded arm.

"You've got a good play behind you," Astrid said. "You know that."

"Think so?" Ivy let her gaze wander into the corners of the ceiling, enjoying the smooth expanse of cream colored paint. "Sometimes I feel that if all the ads were taken away and the publicity stopped, I'd be right back in the middle of hick town."

"You'll get over that. Might take awhile, but it'll go away." Astrid finished her drink in a few gulps. "I know how you feel. As though it's all Colin's doing. Your own talent and work counts for nothing. Propaganda. You think it's all a lie and a fraud."

"Exactly."

"Do this again, will you?" Astrid reached her glass across.

The quinine water made a tangy, refreshing flavor in her mouth. She swallowed the rest of her own drink, feeling a desire to be companionable by keeping up with Astrid. The three dogs and the parrot gave the sensation of company in the room. Somehow she was not alone with the woman. Their bleak solitude was softened by the thumping of a wagging tail against the floor or the sound of feathers ruffled then settled again. She felt quite lovely, being here with Astrid and the pets.

And Astrid wanted her to be here, too. That was rather a compliment.

"You know," Astrid called across the room, "if Colin dropped dead tomorrow, it wouldn't make any difference to your career."

Ivy tilted the gin bottle and watched the liquid flow. "You're exaggerating," she said softly, secretly pleased.

"I certainly am not." There was a pause. "Even if he decided that your career was the worst thing in the world for his own well being, there wouldn't be much he could do about it now."

"Now you are teasing me, Astrid." She couldn't account for the little flutters that had started in her stomach. They tickled pleasurably. She brought the two glasses back to the couch. Astrid took her wrist instead of the proffered glass.

"You have a charming modesty," she said.

She stood quite frozen till Astrid let go.

No one had ever really complimented her sincerely. There was the usual flattery from men who wanted to get her in bed and there had been flights of sporadic enthusiasm from acting professors. Even Mike was tight lipped about voicing his appraisal.

"Thank you," Ivy said, averting her glance.

She occupied herself with the drink, hoping that Astrid would change the subject.

"Modest … and beautiful … and talented. I don't blame Colin for being selfish."

Ivy's embarrassment began to dilute with the growing sensation of pleasure. She respected Astrid. And she knew the woman would not toss words around just for the sake of juggling them. Besides, she thought, studying her half-emptied glass, it was all probably very true.

Ivy sighed. Colin felt very far away. It was delicious just to contemplate the actual distance between them. She snorted a tiny laugh of triumph.

"What are you thinking?" Astrid said.

"How nice it is to be away from Colin. For a change."

"Oh," Astrid's chin tilted downward slightly. "I thought you might say how nice it is … to be here."

"But that's what I meant," Ivy blurted. She twisted at the waist and peered at Astrid, wanting her to see that it was so. "Didn't I come to look for you?"

Astrid poured some more of the liquid down her throat.

Ivy moved a little closer. She put her hand on Astrid's leg and squeezed it. For some reason, she felt it imperative that Astrid believe her.

"Those eyes of yours," Astrid said dreamily. "So blue. So very blue."

Her eyes were beside the point. "Tell me you believe me." She spoke a trifle too loud, her vocal cords lax, all of her not quite steady.

"Certainly I believe you. Why don't you bring that bottle over here and set it on the floor. Then we won't have to run back and forth."

Ivy brought the bottle.

"You know," Astrid continued, "Most young girls have a selfish core. Mean. Destructive." She lifted the bottle and handed it to Ivy. "Destroys all their sex appeal."

Ivy took the bottle. She tried to tilt it steadily over her glass. The two rims bumped together with a sharp clink. Her arms felt very loose at the joints. "Gin is much nicer than whiskey, isn't it?"

"I think so."

"So do I," Ivy repeated. "Kind of sweet smelling on the breath."

"Let's see."

Ivy leaned forward and breathed at Astrid. And Astrid moved right up toward her mouth and kissed her gently on the lips. Ivy blinked.

"Yes, a very sweet breath," Astrid said and relaxed back to the sofa again.

The innocence and casualness with which the kiss had happened disarmed Ivy. She did not know what to make of it. Yet she wasn't angry. And she wasn't upset. She felt suspended in mid-air, waiting for someone to come along and snip the invisible cord so she could float back to earth. She sipped contemplatively at her drink, vaguely tasting the added gin through the quinine water. As she drank, she felt her lips widening into a smile. It was difficult to drink and smile at the same time but she could not seem to control the increasing mirth. She laughed into the glass and heard its hollow, imprisoned sound.

"Something funny?" Astrid said.

She had to put the glass down now and let the laughter roll out. There was nothing funny at all except the laughter itself. She was laughing at herself laughing. She tumbled weakly over beside Astrid and made herself stare at the very close floor until the laughing subsided. She lay there swallowing and feeling weaker. Someone had taken the bones out of her skin and poured in taffy.

She turned her head toward Astrid. Her nose grazed the side of Astrid's breast. She nuzzled her cheek against it, enjoying the downy wool and the resilient mound of flesh beneath.

Somehow the thought of two women together had no relationship to sex. The idea of touching Astrid and being touched by her was like a game. It couldn't produce babies nor be sanctified by marriage. She could hardly take it seriously or be shocked.

"Astrid."

"Hmmm."

"Kiss me again." She braced her chin on the top of Astrid's breast.

"I don't think so."

She knew Astrid was playing. "Why not?"

"You might get to like it."

That would be just fine, Ivy thought with blurred conviction. She tried to stagger up onto her elbows but the weight of her body was much heavier than usual. She felt light in her head and heavy in her chest and none of it made any sense but she didn't care.

"If you don't kiss me," she said thickly, "I'll kiss you."

Astrid grunted a wicked sound of pleasure deep in her throat.

"Well?" Ivy said.

"Well?" Astrid echoed.

"Okay."

With supreme effort and still not quite sure she wouldn't burst out laughing again, Ivy dragged herself up till her face was squarely above Astrid's.

She couldn't maintain the position. She started to laugh slowly as she felt herself beginning to slip down till her lips were tasting Astrid's cool mouth.

Their breasts flattened together.

She felt the curve of Astrid's body aligned beneath her own. She felt her lips being worked apart and Astrid's hands pressing down in the small of her back.

Ivy closed her eyes and the room began to sway, gently, pleasantly. How do women do these things? she wondered without concern.

Then the game began to catch fire. Tremors began to zigzag through her body. She pressed harder against Astrid, needing something to penetrate.

Astrid squirmed out from beneath her and pushed her into the deep cushions. She surrendered herself to the soft probing mouth. It knew where to find the tender spots on her throat.

Dimly she sensed her clothes being removed. A draft of air ran along the inside of her legs. She reached out, needing something to hold onto.

Her eyelids bobbed open. She saw Astrid hunched over her. The short clipped head dove toward her belly.

Ivy's hips lifted off the cushions. "Do something," she muttered, not quite sure what Astrid could do.

Her legs yawned apart. A trickle of perspiration ran around the curve of her buttocks.

She felt a strange contact. A curious sensation made her grip the back of the couch. The material caught beneath her fingernails.

"Inside," Ivy groaned. "Please. Oh, please." She bit her own lip and tried to bear the feeling.

Her body began to shake tremulously.

They almost slid off the couch, but Astrid stiffened and pulled them back.

A sudden point of explosion jolted Ivy into a half sitting position. Her hands clutched the roots of Astrid's hair. The feeling rocked her, destroying all equilibrium. Her eyes grated about in their sockets.

Ivy fell back on the sofa and wiped a trickle of sweat away from the side of her mouth.

She realized that Astrid had gotten off the couch and was kneeling beside her, her forearms lying across Ivy's ribs.

"How are things?" Astrid said.

She wished she felt a little less dizzy. "Fine. Just fine," she murmured.

"But you're in no condition."

"For what?"

There was a silence. "To reciprocate," Astrid said at last.

"But I am," Ivy objected, more out of loyalty than desire.

Astrid patted her chest. "We'll take a raincheck, baby. Anyway, it's time to sober you up."

When the gin had worn off, Ivy realized that not once had she thought of Mike. Not a single time during the whole business.

She decided that gin was much better than whiskey.

And she realized that a hangover at five o'clock in the afternoon was much worse than three hangovers combined at five o'clock in the morning. Her head seemed to be bulging right out of her scalp. The fading gray light of evening made her squint. And she didn't feel quite right, inside. Something had been left feeling lonesome. An unaccountable wave of sadness held her while she got dressed.

She didn't feel right about blaming it on Astrid. Yet she could not deny that what she needed, Astrid could not give her.

They rode back to the theater, sedate, apparently calm. A crazy feeling of half-satisfaction, half-unfulfillment was beginning to shorten Ivy's temper. She felt irritated by the inconvenience of having to go back on stage just now.

The sobering job left her empty and weak. Ivy knew she should eat something but she couldn't take the chance of having it come up on her.

By the end of the first act, she felt cold and sweaty beneath her make-up. She cornered one of the stage hands, gave him a five dollar bill and asked him to get a pint of gin.

He looked from the money to her trembling, nervous fingers. She heard his tongue cluck against the roof of his mouth once. It made Ivy feel ashamed. She didn't want his pity. And she didn't need the reputation of being an alcoholic. Yet she needed something to steady her and the gin seemed the easiest way.

He delivered the bottle to her dressing room. She got the cap off and poured some into a tumbler. Her stomach seemed to open to the liquid gratefully. She gasped and sighed and sat down with the bottle, waiting for the stuff to get a grip on her.

A few minutes later, the machine of her body felt back in working order. Her confidence returned and the sensations of weakness became a facile strength. She dropped the flask into her jacket pocket, feeling a twinge of guilt about drinking during a performance.

The second act went better. She felt a new, invigorating command of her role. Her sense of timing became sharper and she believed that her artistry was soaring to greater heights.

When the show was over, she slopped cold cream on her face and squinted at the red capillaries webbing her eyes. With a greasy hand, she got the bottle out and took another swig, carelessly smearing the cold cream on her jacket. She walked on tricky, springy legs. She wanted to whistle something but couldn't purse her lips quite that finely. She was quite tight.

Ivy wandered down the stage alley and mingled with the Broadway crowds, bumping into people and excusing herself elaborately. A vast blanket of love spread from her to cover the whole city. A pure, spiritual love which changed, as she experienced it, to something else.

Her mouth went slack. She felt the girdle around her hips and cursed its confinement. Someone punched his car horn, then stuck his head out the window and told her to get the hell across the street already. She stumbled up onto the curb and veered into a flower shop. She stood looking about at the flashes of brilliant color, wondering why she had come in. She bought an orchid but couldn't pin it on herself. She bent three pins trying to get them through the suede of her jacket.

The old lady waddled over and helped. She found her wallet, fumbled in it and dropped a flutter of bills to the counter.

Then she was out on the street again, watching a dog sniff at a litter can. The people hurrying by all looked very bundled. Ivy knew it was a windy night. She felt her jacket stirred by the wind but the cold didn't penetrate. She touched the bottle in her pocket and let her fingertips run over the smooth glass.

Astrid. She owed Astrid something, didn't she? She tittered, remembering Astrid's breasts dangling in her face. Great, impassioned performance. Nice little Astrid.

But Astrid didn't have anything in her pants. She didn't have what Ivy needed. And needed right now.

At the corner of Forty second Street, Ivy veered in a wide arc and proceeded beneath the marquees of cheap movie houses where young boys and old men stood talking to each other, while their glances darted at the passing women.

She didn't realize that the man beside her had been sauntering behind her for the past two blocks.

"Hi," he said, touching her lightly on the forearm.

He was wearing tight, dirty white pants. Ivy thought she could see the outline of his athletic support. She forced her glance up to his face. The purple blotches on his skin repelled her.

"Come on," he said. "I'll buy you a drink."

"Bum," she said, annoyed that he made a pass at her so directly. Did she look like a tramp to him?

"Me a bum?" He laughed in a high pitch. "Naw. Not me, sweetie. I got good hard cash." He tapped his pocket suggestively.

All she cared about was the compact line of his hips. She was drunk and dizzy and hard pressed for a man to give it to her. But a remnant of pride needled her and she tried to walk faster to show him she wasn't interested.

He kept beside her easily. "You could go home with some nice change in your pocket."

"Leave me 'lone."

The concrete beneath her feet seemed to have lumps in it. She swallowed hard and tried to clear her vision. He was walking very close to her and she couldn't help bumping into him. The odor of his sweat reached her nostrils. A strong, animal odor that plucked at her senses.

He put his arm around her waist. "You need to have someone look after you."

She knew what she needed. And she knew he was lying through his goddamned rotten teeth. But his arm felt strong and steadying. She wanted to lie down in the gutter with him. Crawl beneath a car.

He steered her into a bar. She let her weight fall heavily on the hard wooden seat. Her body tipped and leaned against the dingy wall. The juke box blared eager, bouncy chords. The stench of beer hung live and hot. He was sitting next to her, crowding her closer to the wall. His hand crept around her armpit and squeezed the side of her breast.

"Whatcha been drinking?" he said.

Her tongue rolled around behind her teeth. The inside of her mouth felt lined with moss. She remembered the crystal taste of quinine water.

"Gin."

"Yeah. Good idea." He leaned out of the booth and called to the bartender.

All she knew was the thick muscles of his thigh pressing against her own. Her leg moved in response.

"You're a pretty girl," he said. The words sounded machine made. "Where you been hiding?"

The bartender brought two shot glasses. She wondered where the quinine water was. But she couldn't form the whole sentence. She could speak quite fluently inside her head but somehow, the words fell apart by the time they reached her lips.

She got the glass to her mouth and she swallowed the little bit in one gulp. It dived for her guts and shook them. Her body clenched, then opened like a morning flower. A focus of pulsation began in the center of each knee cap and started to creep up her legs. Her right hand dropped into the triangle of wood between his legs. She felt the bulge of him against her forearm. He moved his body forward.

They stayed for another round. Then he got her out of the bar and down the street and inside a hotel to his room. She couldn't tell much about the scenery. It swam up and away from her eyeballs.

A heavy odor of dust rose from the mattress as she flopped onto the stained sheets. He pulled the shade and dimmed the steady green blaze of a neon light. As she lay there silently, she could hear it buzz.

The buzzing became part of herself. A growing vibration circled around the base of her spine. The circles grew larger and spread across the lower part of her stomach. She realized it was his hand massaging her.

She lifted her head and let it fall on his knee, turning her face toward the curve of his stomach. "Wanna touch ... wanna feel ..."

His hands moved inside her brassiere and pinched her nipple painfully. She caught her breath and let her teeth sink into the tight sailcloth around his legs. He jumped away.

"Bitch."

"You hurt."

"Broads like to be hurt." He was pressing her shoulders tight to the bed. "They like to be split wide open." He bounced her a little. "Don't they?"

She didn't know. She wanted to be filled with something hard and long enough to choke her.

His hand whizzed through the air and stung her cheek. "Don't they?"

"No."

He whacked her again. She tightened into a little ball against the flaying hands. One breast bounced out of her opened bra. His mouth seemed to hurtle at her. She was too drunk to be frightened, too aroused to give a damn. Pain sparked through her, inciting her passion till it glittered separately alive, divorced from her sanity. She dashed herself against his body, groping for his trousers. He caught her hand and led it down. She sighed and squeezed, moaning crazily.

He flung her onto her belly and yanked down her panties. "No lousy syph broad's gonna..."

A piercing pain made her scream in one long tear of agony. His hand clapped over her mouth. She gasped for breath, furiously shaking her head to free her mouth.

A few moments later, he released her. She wanted to run out of the room, but she could only lie on the bed, panting for breath.

"Aren't you gonna... do it... right?" she said into the pillow.

"Drop dead." He sorted out and tossed a couple of bills beside her cheek. "Now get out of here."

She made herself sit up. All of her felt bruised, her insides broken apart. Yet through the pain, drove the insisting need.

But she knew it was no use here. With him.

# CHAPTER SEVEN

S HE STUMBLED out of the rickety elevator and lurched onto the street, clutching at the grainy walls of buildings to keep herself upright.

A hard core of sobriety began to isolate itself in the back of her head. It spoke to her in a small, steady voice, telling her she had to get sober. The jam and push of Friday night crowds rolled by her and she held herself tight to the wall, afraid to topple into the stream of moving confusion. She stroked fingers through her tangled hair, trying to piece herself together. Got to sober up ... got to ...

Ivy knew she needed help.

She tried to recall Astrid's address. The vision of the hotel mingled with the fluffy red feathers of a parrot. She hiccoughed and lay her cheek against the concrete blocks. Nausea walloped at her chest. She pushed the edge of her forehead to the wall and waited. But it wouldn't come up. Her eyes began to water.

Where was everybody? All her friends? She called Mike a dozen times but he didn't come to her. She clenched her fists and commanded her brain to get sober.

The sensible voice inside her was beginning to get frightened. What if she couldn't get past the haze and the blur? What if she couldn't make it to the theater? Oh God, the theater. Was it curtain time? She pushed her way over-to the light of an Army surplus store and brought the wrist-watch up to her eyes. Almost two o'clock. Had she finished the show? Had she missed it?

She got to the curb and hung onto a mail box till a taxi came around. The driver opened the door for her and she fell in onto the seat.

"Where to?"

She didn't know where she wanted to go. "Home," she said dismally. "Take me home."

"Sure, girlie. Just tell me where you live." His voice was indulgent.

The stark lonesome feeling of her apartment engulfed her. "Madison Avenue..."

They rode along Madison Avenue until the right block swam into view.

She fell into the empty silence and collapsed onto the floor. But she was home. Safe for the moment. She lay still, waiting for the nausea to start again. It rocked up almost to her throat, then subsided. She got herself up from the floor, knowing that she needed water, gallons of water.

She drank from a salad bowl which was sitting on the drain board in the kitchen. A desperate feeling of being all alone on a strange planet blossomed in the silence. She wandered to a chair, put the salad bowl dripping on her lap, and waited to get sober.

She was still sitting there when the telephone jangled through the quiet.

When she picked up the phone, Astrid's voice wanted to know where she'd been all night.

Ivy gazed toward the window and saw that it was morning. A great sweep of relief washed through her.

"Will you come over, Astrid? Please."

She cradled the receiver and yielded to the sweet feeling of being saved.


Astrid, who was seldom shocked by anything, raised her eyebrows in mild surprise at the sight of Ivy.

"Somebody needs a bath," she said, touching a smear of dirt on Ivy's forehead. "Somebody's had one hell of a night."

"Need more than a bath," Ivy said. Her command of sentences had begun to return.

"An ice cold shower would be a good beginning, anyway."

"Nothing's too good for me," Ivy tried to smile. "Did I miss a show?"

"Honey, you don't look like you missed a thing." She was unbuttoning Ivy's smeared jacket. "Not a single thing."

She let herself be stood under the cold spray, her naked shoulders hunching together. Her experiences began to return and line themselves up chronologically.

She stepped out of the shower and let Astrid wrap a towel around her shivering skin. Then she sat down on the closed toilet seat and waited there until Astrid brought in a cup of instant coffee. She needed it to taste thick and sweet. Yet the pungent bitterness felt good to her insides.

"Better?" Astrid said.

Ivy nodded. When she had finished the coffee, Astrid got her to bed and tucked the covers around her.

"You'd better get some sleep before the Saturday crowd tears you to shreds."

"I don't want to sleep," Ivy said, clinging to Astrid's hand. "Don't go away. I've got to tell you ..."

"Tell me later."

She needed to confess all her sins. Apologize to Astrid for what had happened between them. Reveal her shame and her frustration. Listen to good advice from Astrid's years of experience.

But grogginess began to conquer her good intentions. The new mattress held her body gently and she found it difficult to keep her heavy eyelids open.

A stark sleep consumed her.

The shrill voice of an alarm clock yanked her out of the darkness. She got up and called for Astrid. No answer. Then she saw a slip of paper folded beneath the clock.

*Had to go for Shepard. Eat a poached egg and forget yesterday.*

Forget yesterday! Ivy stared at the precisely printed letters, wondering how the woman could be so callous. But, of course, Astrid didn't know. She couldn't know. And she hadn't wanted to listen. A flame of disappointment made her crumple the paper and throw it to the floor. Poached eggs!

She didn't want poached eggs. She wanted a new head. It felt swollen and stiff. It was filled with anxiety and self distrust. She must never never never take another drink.

Which meant she would never be able to enjoy the arms of a man.

She made herself some more coffee, got dressed and went to the theater.

The matinee audience was filled with old ladies who chatted and tittered as though they had come to a tea party. Ivy could feel them out there beyond the lights, pleased with themselves for being in on the latest show and anxious for the performance to be over so they could talk about what they had hardly paid attention to.

Nevertheless she gave of herself. Or what was left of herself beyond the exhaustion, her battered flesh and the growing panic in her mind.

Afterward she submitted to the queries of a few aggressive souls who simply had to come backstage. She allowed them in because she needed to talk. And she needed to hear words of praise. She yearned for something that would annihilate her sense of worthlessness, of waste, of slow destruction.

Then she made herself go to a restaurant and ordered a nourishing meal. She chewed slowly and swallowed with difficulty. Her insides felt raw. The meat felt packed into a corner of her belly. It lay there uncomfortably. But she continued to eat, telling herself she was not about to commit slow suicide just because she couldn't have Mike.

There must be a way to satisfaction. Last night had been a mistake. She'd gone about it all wrong. Without any discrimination. What she needed to do was pick herself a man she could like and put all her efforts into working something out with him.

Certainly not Colin.

It occurred to her that she had an appointment in Connecticut. Ordering more coffee, she sat and pondered the question of Drury Brent. He was intelligent. Attractive in a weird way. Certainly wise.

Disgust at the idea of plotting love made her push away the coffee with dissatisfaction. She needed passion to race after her and catch her up breathless. She had no respect for the cold-blooded approach. It made life empty.

Yet could life be any emptier than it was for her now? She ordered a gin fizz and sipped at it, searching for a way off the merry-go-round.

The evening crowd was better. Some coughing. One sneeze from the second balcony. And lots of applause. She bowed and basked in the clapping. Accepting it like nutriment for her starving soul. Here, on this stage, behind these hot, musty footlights, she possessed identity and worth.

Then she came off into the wings, allowed one of the management to kiss her cheek and made for the dressing room, trying to focus on tonight with Drury and tomorrow with him, too.

She was all set to slam into her car and race up Merritt Parkway when she realized she hadn't seen her car all week.

It was parked downtown. Near Mike's house, she remembered with a shudder.

She didn't want to go into his neighborhood.

She didn't want to be anywhere near him.

But she wouldn't borrow Colin's car. And she was in no mood to ride on trains. Supposing she did go down town? Was it such a big deal? All she had to do was climb out of the taxi and into the Lincoln and drive off. Nothing to make a fuss about.

Yet a strange feeling cooled the heat of her conviction as she got into a cab. She began to wonder if there were such a person as Mike after all. Or did he exist only in the fever of her brain? Had she made him up out of an evil dream? Could anyone who lived and breathed torment her so violently?

She made the taxi driver stop at a liquor store and bought a pint of gin, needing it beside her. Then she got back inside the cab and held the bottle tightly on her lap, not drinking from it, but simply keeping it there for company.

They rode along the crooked streets she had visited so often. Young couples, too loud, too anxious to have a good time before Monday made them subservient again, wavered about in the gutters and milled on corners, unaware, as Ivy was unaware, that it was a biting winter night.

She did not quite recall where she had parked the Lincoln and this was a good excuse to drive past Mike's house. She pressed her face to the window and searched, hoping insanely that he would be coming jauntily down the street, eyes clear, steps sure.

Unconsciously she opened the bottle, cutting through the paper seal with the nail of her thumb. She told the driver to park across the street for a moment. And she simply sat in the back seat, drinking short swallows and gazing at the doorway of Mike's house. She wanted to run out and up the stairs and ... and what?

Yes, she knew dully that there was a Mike. And she was still sober enough to get away.

"All right," she said. "Bleecker and Sixth Avenue."

But she didn't stop drinking. The bottle moved to and from her lips almost without Ivy's knowledge. But she wasn't losing her senses, the way she had the previous night. Instead, she was becoming more and more cool headed. She was seeing the world for what it was. A mumbo-jumbo of stupidity and injustice. Without God. Without beauty.

Her Lincoln was streaked with layers of soot. Leaves had fallen onto the leather seats. She put the key in and turned the motor over, vaguely grateful that it hadn't rained during the week. She blinked carelessly at the needles and saw that the gas tank was half full. Then she wheeled in a swift U-turn and headed vaguely in the direction of Connecticut.

The wind bit her earlobes. But her fingers and toes felt very warm. She raced up First Avenue, enjoying the powerful motor at her command. Playfully, she darted from lane to lane, oblivious to the curses flung at her from cut-off drivers.

She held the wheel lightly with one hand and lifted the bottle with the other. She noticed the stars and began looking for Orion. Someone's brakes screeched.

She laughed at the four letter words flung with exasperation. Then she turned on the radio full force, twisting the dials till she found a symphony. Long-hair music always made her feel brave. Standing up to all those violins and drums and things. She remembered taking a course in music appreciation and listening to the tale of Beethoven's deafness. Brave Beethoven. Imagine composing a whole piece of music and never ever knowing what it sounds like.

The car lurched up from a deep hollow in the road and she hung onto the wheel like the reins of a horse.

The music stopped and a commentator began talking about missiles dropping into the ocean. He sounded very cool about the whole thing. Very precise and uninvolved. Ivy could say long syllabled words in her head but she knew she had gone again past the point of being able to speak them aloud.

She hung onto the steering wheel now and fastened her attention completely on the road. Her hair blew across her face and then away. The thirst for water was beginning to expand. She took another swig of the gin and told herself that pretty soon, Drury would take care of her.

Connecticut sign posts swept by. She read off the names and slowed the car, realizing that she didn't know where the hell in Connecticut Drury lived.

The car bumped off the highway onto a dirt road. The headlights picked out a young boy peddling a two wheeler. She punched the horn. He stopped the bike, letting it fall over to one side, balancing it against a stiff outstretched leg.

"You know Drury Brent?" She rather thought that everyone should know Drury Brent. Good for people. Even children.

The boy pulled his woolen cap off and rerolled the edges.

"There's a Hildagarde Brent t'other side of Westbury."

So she was in Westbury. That called for another drink. She tilted the bottle again and this time emptied it.

The boy pedalled away, hunching his shoulders against the cold.

Maybe Information could tell her the precise whereabouts of the famous Drury Brent.

She drove for awhile, circling about for the center of town. Everything was closed and dark except for the lights of a movie house. After awhile she saw a bar that looked alive. She left the car in the middle of the street and went inside.

The odor of pretzels and whiskey hit her. She felt as though she were swimming around in a large barrel of alcohol that inflamed her eyelids and sent burning fires up her nostrils.

A tiny man on a stool nodded hello to her solemnly. She asked him for a dime. He rummaged through his pockets and brought out a quarter from his vest pocket. It sparkled like a fish eye on the palm of his hand.

Ivy lifted it gently with two fingers and proceeded to the phone booth. She closed the door and got the Operator. But the operator didn't know Drury Brent either. At least she refused to give Ivy his number unless she could tell the address. A silly operator. If she had the address, why would she be calling?

She got long distance and called Astrid.

Astrid was more helpful. It wasn't too far from Westbury, Drury's place. She listened carefully to the directions and repeated them.

Confidently Ivy returned to the car. She found the parkway again and proceeded with extreme caution. Quite sensibly, she did not want to run out of gas. It was two o'clock in the morning.

Drury's cabin was on the side of a hill between four locust trees that waved over it like huge feather boas. A yellow light glimmered behind the porch screen. She parked with a jolting stop and climbed out.

She searched in the dark for a bell, gave up, and knocked hard on the splintery door. She waited, watching fluttery things bang themselves against the screen, trying to get at the light.

Drury had on a checked lumberman's shirt. The cord of his hearing aid seemed more like a misplaced fishing line against the reds and greens.

"I am very tired," Ivy said the words one by one, forming them very carefully. She knew she was very drunk.

Drury seemed to ignore the odor of her breath. He poured her a cup of the blackest, thickest coffee she had ever tasted. But she drank without question.

He had been reading a slim, soft covered volume which he closed now and slipped into a squat bookcase. Then he bent over and started to unlace his boots. When he had gotten them off, he pulled at the heavy woolen socks.

"You look funny in that get-up," Ivy said. She didn't mean to insult him. The words simply popped out.

"And you look beautiful."

She knew he couldn't mean it. Self-consciously she touched her hair and her cheek. Her tongue ran over her lips and felt where the lipstick had melted off or been dissolved by the gin.

A great battle seemed to be waging in her stomach. She swallowed the first urge to retch up its contents.

"Behind you," Drury said.

She made it to the bathroom.

When Ivy came out, she was very sober. "I had a splendid week."

"Apparently."

There was no conversation she could find that was worth Drury's attention. She decided not to speak at all until something intelligent happened into her mind.

"Country folk go to sleep early," he said.

He wanted to go to sleep. They would go to sleep. She hadn't brought pajamas or anything. She felt silly.

"All you need is this nice Indian blanket," he said, reading her thoughts.

He showed her to a second cot in an adjoining room and closed the door between them. She didn't want the door closed. She didn't want Drury to go away and leave her alone. He hadn't talked to her at all. She had disappointed him, coming in drunk and stinking. She had disappointed herself too. But Drury was more important.

Instead of getting undressed, she opened the door and peeked in. He was sitting on the cot, opening the cuffs of his flannel shirt. He looked up.

Ivy pushed the door open all the way. "I just wanted to apologize," she said meekly.

"Apologize? For what?"

She lifted one hand helplessly. "For ... stumbling in."

"Oh, I'm used to that."

She wanted him to be used to it, but not from her. "I don't drink very often."

He smiled now. His eyes seemed to glow against the background of dark and the rustle of the trees. He turned and began to pull the windows shut. They slid down in front of the screen and the room became miraculously silent. "Why do you think I care how often you drink?"

She had no reason. It was conventional to apologize for being inebriated. "All right then. I'm not sorry."

She wanted him to sit her down and worm out of her why she needed to get drunk. She wanted to have a reason for telling Drury everything. Something in the back of her mind was convinced he had a better solution for her troubles. Even if he wouldn't give her the answer, she knew he would give her some kind of solace. Once he'd heard her story.

But she knew that Drury wasn't about to pry. He wasn't Colin. If she wanted to tell him, she'd just have to sit down and tell him, without being asked.

The idea didn't please her residue of pride.

"Drury, I want to talk," she said with effort.

He folded the heavy shirt on a chair seat and went back to the coffee pot. "Yes, I know. I simply thought you would prefer to wait until morning."

"I'd rather get it out of me now. If you don't mind."

He gave her a second cup of coffee, this one less potent. To his own, he added sugar and sat down at the crude table, leaning against the wall and fixing his gaze on her. "Then tell me."

She began to speak with hesitation. There was so much to say, it all crowded out of her at one time. Drury had to stop her occasionally and make her clarify a thought, an episode.

She told him about Mike. About the accident which had taken his sight. And about Colin. And the alcohol.

Drury listened without shock, without surprise. Now and then, he rose to refill her cup or the pot.

It was four thirty before she had finished.

He did not rebound with globs of advice. She wanted him to be brilliant, to produce answers upon demand.

Drury said only one thing: "I think your Mike is a fool."

This was not what she wanted to hear.

"A fool and a coward," he added, seeing her eyes narrow. "And certainly not the hero you make him out to be."

Instantly, she regretted having spoken.

"If you came here for sympathy," Drury said, "you made a long trip for nothing. And," he added evenly, "*that* would disappoint me."

"I thought you could help me understand things I can't seem to figure out for myself." She was sounding like a child and she knew it.

"I see." Drury pushed his feet into a pair of mocassins. "You want me to tell you the source of happy orgasms. The Shangri-La for sex. Thank you for the compliment, but I don't know all that much."

Ivy felt confused. She couldn't comprehend his attitude. Had she been mistaken to feel that Drury was her friend? He neither understood her nor cared to try.

"Perhaps I had better go to sleep now," she said, putting her cup on the wooden wash stand.

"I thought so earlier."

Yet she couldn't leave him. She wanted to grab his shoulders and shake out the words she wanted to hear. "Drury," she said simply, "I don't understand what you're trying to do."

"There is nothing for me to do."

"Of course there is," she blurted. "You know about people. What makes them tick. I'll bet you've known a dozen women with the same trouble. What happened to them, Drury? What's going to happen to me?"

"So now I'm an oracle," he said with a certain pleasant quality. "Lo! the beauties of friendship."

His refusal to share her intensity forced Ivy to be objective. With a flash of insight, she knew what Drury was getting at. She began to see him as he wanted to be seen. A human being, not a prophet or a god. A man who had himself suffered and labored and compromised where life demanded. She realized there was no person exempt from obstacles and conflict. There were only those who could face them and those who couldn't.

"You've helped," she said softly. "You really have."

Drury's smile held affection. "Strange, isn't it?"

Impulsively she leaned over and kissed him on the eyebrow. "Very."

She felt sufficiently calmed to go to sleep.

Bundled in the light warmth of her blanket, Ivy began to think how fortunate she would be if their relationship could develop into something more than being friends. Drury had the stability she needed. Being with him renewed her strength of purpose. She wondered what it would be like to feel Drury's love making.

It took a full minute before Ivy realized that this was her first disloyal feeling to Mike and that she was enjoying it.

The novelty of this kept her wide awake. Novel...and not quite proper.

Yet hadn't she wanted to free herself from a bondage that could never bring happiness?

She felt glad and sad and very curious.

Then she told herself not to dare think that Drury could take her seriously as a lover. Compared to him, she was a mere child. Raw, unmellowed, selfish. And since he knew all her secrets, how could she possibly entice him?

She stared in the darkness at the naked beams across the roof and listened to the occasional creaking of the trees. Drury's protection could pry Mike out of her soul forever. She had to have him.

# CHAPTER EIGHT

THE COUNTRY odor of pine trees and the peaceful seclusion put Ivy to sleep and refreshed her body. She awoke into the morning, bright, resilient and clear-eyed. For a while she lay still on the cot, watching tufts of pure white cloud move across the sky. The crisp smell of bacon frying brought back a healthy appetite. She dressed quickly in the dry cold room and went in to Drury.

She took the spatula out of his hand and turned over the eggs.

She had to show Drury that there were sides of her worth appreciating. And the most obvious start would be her ability to do well in the kitchen. Every man responded to a good cook.

He sat down and folded two napkins on the rugged table. "You had a beautiful sleep," he said conversationally. "The snores rose like organ music."

She knew that he was teasing and that he really meant how much better she looked. Without examining, she felt that the black smudges beneath her eyes had lessened and that the tight lines around her mouth were gone. She was about to quip about the snoring but thought better of it. Even if she did snore, he couldn't have heard it, unless he slept with the bulky hearing aid.

Drury pointed out the dish cabinet and she lay food on two plates and brought them to the table, carrying them in one hand and the coffee pot in the other.

"You used to be a waitress," he said, noting her agility.

"I used to be everything," she laughed.

During breakfast she told him about the carefree days when nothing was too difficult so long as there was a promise of a part sometime in the future. The nostalgia made her speak fluidly and at length. Those were the days before Mike, of comparative innocence, of dreams yet to be lived.

She was still speaking when a delivery boy rode up the dirt path and dropped a newspaper on the doorstep.

"I like to read about New York at a distance," Drury said as he went to bring the paper in.

Ivy cleared the table and washed the breakfast things while Drury took out one section of the paper and began leafing through. She felt cozy and very like Sunday morning for real. The secure feeling reached down through her, grasped the desperate passion and crumpled it to nothingness. How lovely it would be if she could conquer the raging lust that drove her to stupidities. There were many women, married women too, who went through life without being satisfied. Somehow, they managed without going berserk. They raised families and maintained a healthy home. Why couldn't she be one of them?

Why, indeed.

But though she spoke these words to herself, Ivy knew she could never be one of these women who lived a half life, a gray placid existence. She could never be happy with substitute contentments. Her body was no servant to intellectual commandments. She needed love. She needed ecstasy. Those thrilling moments of animal fury were the real reasons for living.

She heard Drury snort behind the newspaper. She turned, curious, and saw him flinging it onto the table. His eyes narrowed into slits of angry yellow. He flicked at the cord of his hearing aid for an instant, preoccupied with a thought.

"Something?" Ivy said.

"Nothing much."

She watched him control the agitation. "Come on, what is it?" Ivy stayed across the room, hesitating to step into the aura of his concern. She began to feel a little nervous, watching his lips draw back slightly against his teeth.

"You know people do just about anything to earn a living," he said. "Nobody takes them seriously all the time."

Ivy sensed that he was composing a nice prologue for her. "You were reading the gossip column, weren't you?"

She saw she had struck home.

"All right," he said with decision. "You're going to hear it from somebody. Might as well get it over with. But first promise me you're not going to take this blood sucking seriously."

Ivy nodded. She came over and put herself into a chair, feeling a tiny quaver in her neck.

Drury opened the paper again. He began reading.

*What rising young comet has been shooting off her fires at the world's crossroads? Fires lit by alcohol, that is. We prefer our blondes aloof and stately. Or at least discreet. Comets rise and fall in an instant. Pity.*

She grabbed the paper out of Drury's hands and read it for herself.

"One reads that sort of thing about everyone," Drury said. "Let's take it lightly."

Ivy clutched the paper and held it stretched out between them. "But it's true," she said. "He didn't make it up!"

"So it's true. Your video spot tonight will squash this thing flat."

"Drury, you're being kind, aren't you?"

"I think what's more important is how you conduct yourself in the future."

He was absolutely right and that was what frightened Ivy more than the actual squib. How could she guarantee to behave herself? When desire surged through her flesh, she was helpless. When her thighs began to pulse and her back stiffened, could she ignore it? Could she lock herself inside the house like a bitch in heat? She leaned over and put her head in Drury's lap.

"You've got to help me," she whispered. "Please."

His comforting hand stroked through her hair. "You've been fortunate so far. Perhaps you'll continue being fortunate. God protects madmen and drunkards, after all."

"And I'm both."

"So are many of your colleagues, though who would know it when they're shining on stage? If you're afraid that this thing is bigger than you are, I suppose all you can do is learn to live with it."

She reached up and entwined her fingers in his. "But I don't want to lose my career. I don't." Ivy swallowed to choke a sob.

"Of course you don't. But why should you if you continue to fill your obligations on stage? I'm one of those old fashioned fogies who believes that a person's private life should be just that. Private."

He was telling her gently, kindly that it was her responsibility to do her drinking, and her whoring, behind closed doors. But this was like telling her to sail a boat without water. She didn't choose when to get drunk. She didn't chose to pick up strange men and make a spectacle of herself. If this decision depended on her own good sense, she would cut out the lower part of her body and have done with it once and for all.

"The next time, it'll be worse, won't it?" she said.

"Oh, he won't use any names. Don't worry about that." Drury cupped his hands around her cheeks and lifted her face. "Now dry those tears. Your friend Mr. Denny won't take this lying down."

She realized that when she got back to New York she would have to face more than Ed Denny. Colin would be around, demanding explanations. And Astrid would have her share of silken words to gloss over this thing with casual, biting cynicism.

And maybe her family would read it. What could she say to Leo if he asked questions?

Ivy wished she were dead.

She sat very still while Drury blotted her cheeks with a clean napkin.

"You have a show tonight. We'd better start getting back to the city."

Since her Lincoln had no gas, they decided to drive back in Drury's station wagon and send somebody up to collect her car later. Ivy helped him close the house and they talked about all the trivia of country living as though the thing which had happened to Ivy were not worth further notice.

She had no choice but to share Drury's confidence that she could manage to control her behavior.

He drove the station wagon slowly. It was an old vehicle that he liked to tinker with. "Don't let the bounces scare you," he said. "It needs some new shocks ... shock absorbers, in the rear."

Ivy asked him about carburetors and points to keep him talking so her mind would be free to go over and over the jolting experience. She could not let go, hypnotized by the immensity of the humiliation.

"You aren't listening, Ivy."

She put her hand out to the wind and let it sift icily through her fingers. "I can't think straight either." Her tone was flat. "I feel drugged."

"Is it really that bad?" He pulled out the ash tray for her. "I mean, this emphasis on sex. Maybe you've built it up out of fright. Scared yourself with a boogieman."

Ivy whirled on him with indignation. "Do you think I would jeopardize my whole life with something I ... I made up?"

He leaned over the wheel to scratch a spot off the windshield. "Lots of people do. And I think you've had more opportunity than most."

His words made her boil. "Would *you* like to try?" Her voice was too loud.

"Now wait a minute." He lifted his shoulders against her anger. "I was merely asking a question."

"All right. I'm asking you a question too."

Ivy's feminine strategy was working without her knowing. Dimly she knew that she was challenging Drury's prowess as a male. Experience had taught her that this kind of attack was irresistible. And if she could keep Drury on tap, it would save her from making a public fool of herself on the streets.

"Well?" Ivy said.

"I'm no good at experiments."

She sat back against the seat and folded her arms, sensing that Drury was turning the idea over. After all, she was young, much younger than he. Obviously passionate. Attractive to him, though he managed to keep this well hidden. Would he really let the opportunity slip by? Ivy doubted this.

He let her off at Madison Avenue in time for her to shower and dress for the evening.

"I'll watch the show," he said, pulling the door shut.

"Will you call me tomorrow? Just for reassurance?"

Drury adjusted the rear view mirror. "If it'll save you a night's sleep, why don't you phone me after the show?"

"I'll do that."

She went upstairs, feeling a slight touch of triumph.

Ivy locked the door, resigning herself to the unpleasantness of getting in touch with Colin.

He lifted the receiver before the first ring ended. From the tenseness of his voice, she knew he'd been sitting by that phone all day. He didn't have to mention the newspaper item. It ran a nasty undercurrent beneath his politeness.

Then she took a warm shower, knowing he'd be over to rave at her all during the time she got dressed. She decided that if Colin became too much of a nuisance, she would tell him to go to hell.

He kept his finger on the doorbell till she got a robe hastily around her and answered. In case she hadn't read it, he was carrying the paper with him.

"I saw it, Colin. So don't bother me." She lifted the damp curls off her neck and trailed back to her dressing table.

He came in and sat down on the edge of the bed. "Don't bother you? What do you mean, don't bother you?" He slapped the paper on his knee. "Do you think I'm going to stand for this? Am I an idiot to let you run around? Trust you?"

"Oh, come off it." Guilt was feeding her with deadly ammunition. At any moment, the words would spill over her lips, telling him that he had never owned her. That he had never even really possessed her.

"I think you're having a nervous breakdown. Look at this place."

Surprised, she looked around the room. For all her playing with the furniture, the room looked slightly atilt. The rugs and curtains clashed in shades of pink. The lamps on either side of the bed were out of balance. All her preoccupation and her insecurity were obvious.

"I don't have time," she said, painfully bringing her eyes back to the reflection of her face in the dressing table mirror.

"No, I guess you don't," he said cuttingly.

Ivy made herself think about the lipstick brush and the application of mascara and eye shadow which all required a delicate touch from a steady hand.

"I'll tell you this much, my dear friend," he bounced up from the bed and came to stand over her. "If I didn't have an investment in you, I'd drop you right back into that dirty little hole where you seem to belong anyway."

"Colin, shut up. Sit down in the living room and just shut up till I'm ready to leave." Her voice was steady and hard. She heard him exhale through his mouth and felt the large bulk of him tighten.

"You're insane," he breathed.

But he went into the living room.

Ivy began to brush her hair, relieving her anger in vigorous strokes that made her scalp tingle. She wished she could be certain that Drury would have her now that she had bounced herself free of Colin. She needed that feeling of a man within reach who loved her and wanted to take care of her. All the competence she had was restricted to her performance on stage. Away from the theater, she was a floundering duck who didn't have enough sense to come in out of the rain. And things were getting tougher all the time.

She wondered how low she could bounce.

Methodically she pomaded her hair into an upsweep and pinned a spray of garnet into the wave. The deep red stones and the pale blue wrap-around gown were fire and ice. Her luminous eyes beneath the high arched brows defied anyone to believe the columnist's gossip. She would play her arrogance to the hilt. Drury would be proud of her. And because of what he knew, he would fall in love with her. Yes, Colin could definitely go to hell.

Carrying an ermine stole over her forearm, she went into the living room.

"I'm ready now," she said.

The promise of Drury made her ready for anything.

In the Rolls, Colin sat as far away from her as he could manage. Ivy laughed to herself, knowing that he wouldn't be able to resist putting on an intimate show when they reached the studio. He couldn't admit to the world that Ivy had made a fool out of him. And his pretense of loving attention would kill the destructive rumors. Poor Colin. She had him coming and going.

The rehearsal was just a quick scanning of some cue lines, a half hour before the show. Last minutes commotions were centered on the big acts and on continuity. Everyone was too busy to care about the latest gossip concerning Ivy Sherwood.

When the cameras panned to her, Ivy smiled into their polished convex lenses. She carried herself glamorously but spoke with modest understatement for the thousands of viewers watching her on the coast to coast hook-up. Not all of them had read the column and certainly fewer would understand that the paragraph was meant for her.

She still had a chance. There was yet reason enough for optimism.

When her stint was over, she let Colin escort her outside.

"Don't bother taking me home," she said as his hand fell away from her arm.

Colin's performance had been almost as good as her own. "I didn't expect to," he answered. "No doubt you have an appointment with some handsome wino."

Her hand started up to slap his face but stopped and clung to the ermine.

"You can't afford to make a scene," Colin said softly.

It was true and she knew it.

"And from now on, you can conduct your business directly with Ed. He's got a stronger stomach."

She let Colin have the last word, glad to be rid of him, glad to have done with the sickening pretense.

Without further comment, Ivy got into a cab, her mind already occupied with Drury.

In the taxi she decided to call him from her home. Perhaps she could get him to come over. The decorating job would shock him, but not in the same way it had upset Colin. No, Drury would realize the furnishing to be one more symptom of her need for his emotional support.

She settled herself comfortably in a deep chair and dialled Drury's number.

It took no doing at all to convince him to accept her invitation.

She hung up the receiver, wondering whether it would be best to change into a simple dress or slacks and a sweater or a casually revealing negligee. A flutter of nervousness made her change twice before she felt content with her appearance. The camel colored wool dress looked sedate enough. There was no point to flaunting her designs on him.

But there was neither shame nor guilt in her heart as she thought about seducing Drury. In her isolation and fear, she needed him sincerely. He had the magic words of comfort. And she was so lost among the welter of conflicting desires that Drury was a miracle from heaven for her.

Most of all, she wanted desperately to be good. To confine her explosions of desire to the privacy of his arms alone. She ran a comb quickly through her hair, letting the upsweep fall into a soft pattern of waves about her shoulders. Then Ivy stared at her face, telling herself over and over that he wanted her. That she was attractive to him. Her self-confidence ebbed and surged with doubts, then lifted her out of despair and into the promise of decency.

She let Drury in and watched his reaction to the scarlet cabinets and the black rug with its blue-green dragons.

"Sprightly here," Drury said, dropping his homburg on a long mosaic table. "You were wonderful tonight. Carried it off like Garbo herself."

"Thank you, Drury. I wouldn't believe anyone but you."

She switched one of the Japanese lanterns a bit lower.

"You're feeling better, I see."

"Yes. I ended it with Colin." A smile flashed across her lips. "That was a big help."

"I should think so."

Ivy didn't quite know how to cut the formality. They had been so relaxed together in Connecticut. Why didn't it happen now? Was he wary of her challenge? Did he expect her to leap on him?

She surveyed him, letting her mind wander to how those quick, graceful fingers might probe her body. How he would look beneath the formal lapels of his striped gray suit.

"Shall we have some coffee?"

"That would be good." He opened his jacket and sat down, pulling up his trousers at the creases.

Ivy went into the kitchen and put up water. Perhaps he was purposely keeping distance between them. The lure of this began to excite her. She was not accustomed to a man who could take his time. With Mike, it had been a breathless grabbing. Sometimes they couldn't wait long enough to reach the bedroom.

And there sat Drury, all ease and relaxation. It made her blood rise and pound in her chest. She pressed herself against the cold refrigerator to cool off her burning skin. Her ankles felt weak and a spidery, ticklish sensation rose along the backs of her legs.

Suddenly, she wanted a drink.

Ivy flung open the cabinets and stared at the bare shelves. She knew there wasn't a drop of gin or whiskey in the whole damn apartment. And Drury certainly hadn't brought any.

The old, clammy dread began to grip her. It was going to be the same thing all over again. Her insides crying and screaming for it. Her body thrashing her against him without hope of fulfillment. She balled her fingers into futile fists of despair.

The kettle began to sing in a high thin voice. She put cups on saucers, the china clattering in her grasp. Then she splashed the water over the instant mix and put cream and sugar on a tray. She couldn't let Drury know her condition.

But she had been honest with him so far. This honesty was precious to her. What was the use of trying to fool him? In the end it would turn out that she was only fooling herself. If she had any faith that Drury could help her, she had to let him know how she felt. Shame slithered into red spots of color in her cheeks.

She brought the tray in and set it down beside his homburg, moving the hat carefully to the edge of the table.

"What is it?" Drury said as her trembling hands began to maneuver the cream.

"You know what it is," she answered without looking at him.

He didn't reply.

"And it's all for you," she said in a softer voice. "Not just any-one, Drury. Only you."

Still no answer.

"I mean that."

She felt the courage now to look at him, knowing that all she was feeling lay revealed in her eyes. "Could you want me?"

He lifted her away from the table and made her sit down beside him. But he kept his hands carefully away from the intimate spots of her body.

"I don't think there's a chance if we get started on this track."

She had been so direct that there was no room left for hedging. "It wouldn't interfere with our friendship. We aren't children."

"I don't want to disappoint you."

She respected the truth of this but it couldn't persuade her. "You don't have to." She spoke carefully, not wanting to insult him by the suggestion her words held. If he cared at all for her welfare, he would go out and get her a bottle. That would solve everything.

Drury understood the look in her eyes. "Is that really what you want?"

"Yes," she said, hating herself, yet eager for the release he could bring to her. "It's no reflection on you. Only myself."

"Thank you for being so considerate of my pride," he said matter-of-factly.

She bent close and kissed him on the lips, her own slightly parted. Her fingers played lightly beneath his ear. Crazily, she wondered if he would take the apparatus off before making love. "I really want you," she whispered against the side of his mouth. "And if there were any other way..."

His hands moved irresistably along the neckline of her dress. "Won't you try?"

The remembrance of all her failures throbbed in her temples. "Don't ask me to do that," she pleaded. "You can't know the pain."

"We'll make a bargain." He was beginning to breath heavily. Ivy knew he would do anything she wanted. She snuggled closer and pressed herself against his sleeve.

"Whatever you say, my darling." She ran the point of her tongue to the edge of his eyelid and felt his body shudder. Her own flesh kindled in response.

"I'll get your bottle. But promise me you won't touch it unless it's ... absolutely necessary."

"Of course."

She managed to let go of him so he could get up and out quickly before their passion went too far.

While he was out, she changed into a pink negligee which filmed her breasts and made all her body a delicate rose hue. It was going to be all right. Drury understood her. He was sensitive to what she needed. Their union would be a success.

Hope, hope at last. She lay down on the bed and spread her limbs wide, feeling the gauzy material sink between her naked thighs. Visions of male and female raced across her brain. Anticipating the joy, she lifted her hips and began a swinging, circular motion that egged on her desire.

The doorbell rang. In her hurry, she had let the lock snap shut. She got off the bed and ran eagerly, barefoot, to the door.

Drury's glance slid over her. He stepped inside the door and brought her tightly to him.

Holding onto him, she stepped backward, leading them gradually into the bedroom.

He sat her down on the bed and put the package on the nighttable. Then he took off his clothes and hung them neatly on a spare hanger. Ivy watched his movements attentively, eager to know his nakedness with her eyes as well as her touch. He undid the hearing aid and slipped it into his pocket.

"Yes," he said, anticipating her thought. "I am almost totally deaf. But I can read leaps with my eyes and with my fingers. So don't let it bother you." He enunciated the words with precision as though adjusting their volume with a dial inside his head.

He was square and compact and extremely virile. Ivy smiled, closed her eyes and waited for Drury to come to her.

His fingers began to tease and meander, playing slowly, subtly with her. She rubbed against him a little and touched him in return, savoring his presence. She told herself she would not speak at all. They would do everything with hands and knees and toes and bodies. They wouldn't need words.

They lay together on their sides, feeling each other lightly, drawing out each sensation, exploring flesh and fat and muscle. He moved one leg between her thighs and began to draw it back and forth till her own legs gripped his and held tightly. His mouth circled beneath her breasts and she felt the flatness of his tongue draw up points of skin, while his body readied her for penetration.

Her hands groped to hold him. Small convulsions began to move her to the extremes of readiness. She could not curb the anxious feeling of wanting him to be inside her. Her legs crept farther outward. One foot hung off the mattress. A fire engine clanged down the street, piercing the night and she shivered, knowing that Drury couldn't hear it.

"Give it to me, baby," she said, believing that he could not tell that she spoke and feeling, therefore, a certain obscene freedom.

But the vibrations carried down through her body and his fingers went up to her lips.

"I could love you," she said. And Drury patted her ear in reply.

His languidness began to quicken. He put his arms beneath her back and arched her belly to his lips. His tongue fluttered and caught her at the side of her waist. She felt his soft hair moving downward. Her hips thrust at him, urging him. This way drove her crazy.

"In," she panted. "Put it in."

He didn't have to touch her lips to know her meaning. He rose above her and sank down hard between her legs. She gasped and one hand groped fearfully for the bottle. She could not bear to chance the abating of her feeling. She struggled with the bottle cap while her body moved in rapid rhythm with his own. She gulped down large swallows of gin, coughing and choking. It ran over the sides of her mouth and her throat seared, but she prayed to get drunk quickly.

The dizzy feeling of confidence rolled over her. She dropped the bottle to the carpet where it bounced softly and lay still as half the remaining liquid slopped out.

Ivy sighed and grabbed him anew. The door to escape felt wide open. She felt his fingers slipping in the perspiration of her back. How delicious he felt, jamming with hard, persistent force.

"Deeper," she groaned. "Kill me."

She clung fast and raced on, tangling in the blanket, sliding together. He knew how to do the thing. She bit his ear, wanting it to go on forever.

She could tell that he was hungry too—hungrier, if possible, than herself. They shuddered and clung. But once was not enough for either of them.

He rested a moment beside her, then began again. Secretly she blessed him.

For hours they drained and filled and redrained each other, changing positions as muscles started to ache.

"Oooh...I'm gonna keep you," she said from between lips swollen and dry with gin. "Gonna love you up..." Words muttered and mingled with saliva.

Exhausted, they fell asleep. Then woke again and came together in the midst of half dreams. A long, long time since she'd had it so good. Every tendon felt strained to the limit. Blood marks were alive all over her body. Together they were insatiable, perfect, complete until eternity.

The demands of Drury's job made them stop at daylight. While he took a shower, Ivy lay hugging the pillow and thinking back on it all with disbelief. She couldn't tell whether she were sober or drunk. But not since Mike's blindness had she been happier.

Drury had taken his clothes into the bathroom and he came out now fully dressed. He bent over and picked up the bottle. She saw a tone of sadness slacken the corner of his mouth.

"You were perfect," she breathed. "I love you and you were perfect."

He set the empty bottle on the bed. "Not quite."

It didn't really matter to her about the alcohol.

Drury leaned over and kissed her good-bye.

"When will I see you?" she said, holding onto his collar.

"I'll ring you up after tonight's show."

She sighed happily and drifted back into sleep. Still half drunk, it was simple for her to believe that all her troubles had been solved.

# CHAPTER NINE

Her experience with Drury felt like an act of salvation. Through the hangover, which rattled about in her throbbing head and queasy stomach, came a sense of well being. She dressed rapidly and decided to walk to the theater.

Filled with a thrilling energy, Ivy strode the long blocks. Lunch hour crowds were emptying from office buildings. Whiffs of delicatessen and char-broiled hamburgers mingled with the traffic odors of gasoline exhaust fumes. On a whim she pushed into the crowd lined up at a hot dog counter. How long since she'd felt human enough to take part in normal every-day living.

Ivy bit into the frank with relish, but after a few swallows she realized that her stomach didn't want this. Nervously she lit a cigarette and went back onto the avenue. It was too early in the day for gin, but already her stomach craved it. She had no business feeling the need for a drink. Besides, she had no reason just now. There was a show to do. She inhaled the nicotine deeply and held it in her lungs. She felt her palms beginning to perspire. When she reached the theater, all of her felt alive with nameless irritation.

She put her make-up on quickly and changed into costume, determined not to give in. She drank three glassfuls of water, hoping to fill the shaking emptiness.

Then she went on stage. The spotlighting in the second act felt as though it would burn right through her.

During intermission she sent out for a bottle, promising herself to take just enough to see her through the rest of the performance.

She began to feel steadier after one short swallow.

When the last curtain fell, Ivy's good intentions had disappeared. All she knew was the growing thirst inside her.

She closed the dressing room door and lifted the bottle to her lips. Her body shuddered and sighed. A bead of perspiration trickled down the curve of her nose. She gasped and winced and continued to drink hungrily.

A knock at the door made her swing the bottle behind her back instinctively. "Just a moment." Her voice sounded rough. She screwed the cap back on and slipped the bottle into a drawer.

The wardrobe mistress came in. "There's a lady outside says you'll be wanting to see her." She handed Ivy a note.

Her first thought was a pang of conscience. Must be her mother coming to find out why she hadn't been in touch with the family all this time.

Ivy unfolded the paper. The name scrawled on it made her tighten and grow cold. "I'll see her."

She stood beside the mirror and tried to seem nonchalant as Hilda sauntered in.

"You got a nice show, Miss Sherwood," Hilda said. The thin lips wangled her bony face into a smirk. She set a battered bulging case beside her ankle.

"What do you want?"

Hilda came further into the room and sat down at the dressing table. "There I was, sittin' in my little apartment watching television ..." Hilda's voice trailed away as she touched her coarse curls inspectingly. "You got a nice, fancy arrangement. All kindsa friends. Boy friends too, I'll bet."

"I said what do you want?" Ivy formed the words precisely, trying not to betray her own uneasiness.

"What do I want?" She turned away from the mirror now and narrowed her gaze on Ivy's reddened lids. "Well, I don't want a drink. That's for sure."

"You'd better speak up or get out. I've no time…"

"You got plenty of time, Miss Big Shot. Don't you try foolin' me with this high falutin' talk. I ain't one of your starry eyed fans, y'know. And what I could tell 'em wouldn't do your reputation much good either." She paused for breath, satisfied by her own importance.

The implication of blackmail rang heavily in Ivy's ears. She would rather be smeared across the front pages of all the tabloids than pay this hag one cent. She stared at the coarse, ugly make-up, knowing that Mike kissed this face, held this wretched body in his arms. She wanted to cry for the Mike that had once been.

"I ain't come for handouts, if that's what you're think-in'." Hilda said. She got up and dragged the case over to the stool. "I just thought y'might be appreciative."

Hilda unsnapped the tarnished lock. She lifted the lid and took out sculptured terra cotta. The head resembled Ivy's strangely.

"Wouldn't ya like to buy a few things done by your ex-lover?"

Ivy grabbed the work, not wanting it to be touched by Hilda's dirty hands. "How did you get this?"

"He gives 'em away. Kinda pretty, huh? I figure they must be worth plenty more than *he* thinks. 'Specially to you. So I thought I'd just bring 'em along."

It was indeed a tactful form of blackmail, Ivy knew. But what Hilda didn't know was that she would certainly pay any price to own Mike's work. Cautiously she peered into the valise. There were half a dozen studies of hands and torsos. Each of them bore a likeness to her own body. A rush of sadness dimmed her. Was Mike's recollected vision of the world revolving around herself? Was he thinking of her as his fingers formed the clay?

"I'll take them all," Ivy said, not caring to be shrewd. "How much?"

Hilda shifted uneasily and one eyebrow twitched in surprise. "There's six of them there. Fifty dollars each should be a bargain to you." She studied Ivy to see how the price set. "Or maybe I'll be nice and give you the whole lot for a flat two hundred."

Ivy examined into her purse. "I've got twenty five dollars."

"That's okay," Hilda said, snapping the money. "You can write me out a check for the rest. Make it to cash."

"I don't have a check book with me."

"Then we can go along to your apartment."

Hilda's persistence made Ivy consider. If Mike continued to sculpt, she would be back again. And each time the price would go up, of course.

"You'd better settle for the twenty five," Ivy said. "Or there might not be any future in this business for you." She watched Hilda think this through.

Hilda rolled up the bills and stuck them into her blouse. "I just got a kind heart."

After she left Ivy bent over Mike's work and lifted each piece out carefully. Her hands shook with excitement. How Mike would curse if he knew what had happened. She sat fondling the statuary, turning it around and around on her dressing table. Through her prejudice in Mike's favor, she could see that they were good. Emotional, direct and clean of line. His fingers saw with a clarity of vision that must command respect. She sat back and read each statue as though it were a love letter written to her. For there was no doubt but that she was the persistent theme of his work.

And his love for her was helping Mike to build himself a new future.

The thought overwhelmed Ivy. She brought out the bottle and began again to drink, wanting to drown away her sudden urge to run to Mike.

After awhile the world blurred and became pleasantly dull. She put the works back into the valise and wandered out to look for a cab.

When Ivy got home, she placed the sculptures variously around the living room, then called the local package store and ordered a case of gin.

She sat in the middle of the floor, drinking and believing in Mike's future and seeing it all so very clearly without herself. When Drury came, he would see the work and know that Mike was not the coward he thought.

Dear Drury. She wanted him to come over right now and hold her in his arms. Tell her all the right things to drive out the loneliness.

She called him at home and then at the office and pleaded with him to come over right away. She couldn't wait until tonight to see him. She needed him … now.

She refused to hang up till he said yes.

Drury came in and she staggered to him, flung her arms around his neck and clung tight, squeezing hard against the reality of his strong body.

He kissed her forehead and stroked her temples. His touch inflamed her. The whirlpool of passion would dissolve her thoughts about Mike. She began to rub herself against Drury, fondling him and pulling him down with her to the floor.

"I need you to make love to me. Hold me tight, darling. Hold me."

Breathlessly she rubbed her mouth against his cheek and nuzzled her face against his shirt collar, smearing lipstick carelessly on it. "I can't stand to be away from you. Not a minute. Not a second." She was beginning to mutter incoherently.

Drury tried to hold her away. But she forced herself close to him, needing to hide inside his flesh, searching to escape from pursuing thoughts of hopeless depression.

"Ivy, get hold of yourself."

"I don't want to. I want you to get hold of me." She laughed a little and kicked off one shoe. "I want us to bum with one flame."

"That's a line from your play," he said.

Ivy felt he wasn't cooperating. She didn't like the stiffness in his shoulders. He seemed annoyed. "I can make you happy," she persisted. "You know I can."

Drury cradled her head in his arm. "I wish you could make yourself happy."

"Please be nice."

She didn't want him to talk any more. Words and thoughts disturbed her. Ivy lifted herself up with a sudden movement and pushed him down to the carpet. Whether or not he wanted it, she was going to force Drury to make love to her.

But he was too strong. He held her body at arm's length as she struggled to get close.

"You've got to sober up," he said. "This is ridiculous."

He lifted her into his arms and carried her, kicking and struggling, to the bathroom. She let him take her clothes off, thinking that her nakedness would entice him to other things. But he paid no attention to her heaving breasts as she tried to flaunt them in his face. Holding her tightly with one arm, he managed to get the cold water running in the tub.

She screamed and tried to bite. But he dumped her in. The water splashed over his suit. She caught him with her wet hands and tried to pull him into the tub with her. She spat water all over his shirt and waves of it flowed over the side. But she couldn't conquer him.

Ivy quieted and lay shivering in the water. Her senses began to return and brought with them a hot feeling of shame.

Drury sat down on the toilet seat and removed his jacket. She watched him transfer the hearing mechanism to his shirt pocket.

For awhile she lay meekly still. Then she said, "I guess I should be sorry."

"You ought to be something," Drury said. "Concern for your own welfare would be more appropriate than sorrow."

Ivy realized that out of the three times they'd seen each other, she'd been sober only once. She stepped out onto the bathmat and put a towel around her dripping body. "Please forgive me, Drury. I get lost sometimes, that's all."

She dried herself quietly and put on a fresh dress. They went back into the living room and dragged the case of gin out of sight.

Drury's glance fell on one of the pieces of sculpture. He strolled over and inspected it closely. "Where'd you get this?"

"A friend." Ivy's heart began to pound. "Do you like it?"

"Has a definite flair. Is it…"

"Mike's? Yes."

Drury paused, fingering the top of the statuary. "I didn't know you'd been seeing him." His voice was a trifle strained.

Ivy noticed the disappointment. "I haven't been," she said, "I told you I wasn't ever going to see him again. And I don't intend to."

Drury turned and surveyed her, waiting for the rest of her explanation.

She told him the episode with Hilda.

"Well, for twenty five dollars, you didn't go wrong." He tried to laugh.

"You mean they are worth more, aren't they?" Her eyes sought his eagerly.

He rolled down his sleeves to let the wet spots air. "Let's not be over anxious, my dear. His work shows promise, yes. But what he does with it, how he develops… One role doesn't make an actress and a few pieces of sculpture don't make an artist. We'll have to see what happens."

Ivy came over and squeezed both his wrists. "But the chances are good?"

"Very."

A smile of pride beamed in her eyes. "I know he'll keep working. And Hilda knows she can get money out of me, so she'll bring me his work for sure. Is there anything we can do, Drury, to help him sell?"

He unfastened her grasp and put his hands on her shoulders. "I want you to remember one thing, Ivy. The man is blind. His progress, therefore, is limited. A fine amateur, yes. But a professional, serious artist I would not hope for, if I were you."

His words did not daunt her. As long as Mike could touch things and see them through his fingers, as long as he wanted to sculpt... That was the important part.

"May I keep showing you his work?"

"By all means," Drury said. "And if it continues to improve, I'll help you sell it."

"Oh, Drury," she kissed him hard on the side of his mouth. "I love you so!"

Her thoughts leapt ahead to one man shows for Mike, his fame and fortune as a sculptor. She wished she could call him and share her dreams and the good news of Drury's approval.

"I'd better go home and change these clothes," Drury said.

She let him go, not realizing that Drury wanted to leave her alone with her plans that could never include him.

Ivy spent awhile reminding herself that she must not get in touch with Mike. The temptation nagged at her, pulling her over to the telephone every so often. To speak with him for just a few minutes. To encourage him, tell him of her faith.

But Mike would not welcome such a call. He would be angry that she was making such a big thing so prematurely. He would feel that she was butting her nose in where it didn't belong. And, most likely, he would demand the pieces back.

Ivy had no intention of parting with them. It was almost like having Mike with her in this very room. Not the bitter recluse he had become. But the talented, ambitious person with whom she had first fallen in love.

For awhile she sat quietly and smoked cigarettes, letting her gaze devour the symbols of him. Feeling his presence and his love. What better expression of love could there be than these images of herself done in miniature...

The temptation to call him faded. Now that he was working again, doing something of use, she had to let him alone more than ever. With her belief in Mike's eventual success grew also the belief that he would come to feel worthy in his own mind. And when he did feel worthy, then he would call her.

She had to trust this.

In the meantime, she felt a great urge to show him off. She went to the phone now and called Astrid, wanting her to see and admire. To praise... and perhaps to buy.

She could not be so cautious as Drury.

When Astrid came in, Ivy saw that her invitation had been misinterpreted.

She tilted Ivy's chin and kissed her casually on the lips, feigning that blase attitude necessary for successsful excursions into the back roads of love.

Ivy let the kiss happen without comment. She did not want to hurt Astrid's feelings. Nor did she wish to become involved with her again. Despite the afternoon's misadventure, she felt content with Drury. Her stimulated senses were looking forward to spending the night with him again... and again.

Astrid said, "You do better when the gas tank's filled, don't you, honey?"

"Always," Ivy laughed. But she was not about to guzzle any more gin.

"Well then?" Astrid dropped her coat over the arm of the couch and patted her ribs. "I could do with a little something myself. The show's closing in two weeks, you know. And I'm off to Hollywood for some high flying. Got to get in practice."

"No, I didn't know," Ivy said, stalling for time. She did not trust herself to share so much as one sociable drink. The thermostat of her body seemed to jump its temperature at the first swallow. And she felt rocky enough for one person.

"I hope you'll take a peek in on Shepard now and then. He has a nasty way of getting sentimental." She came over and touched her nose to Ivy's. "Not at all like you, my pet."

"I'll miss you," Ivy said, leaning away from the curving glossy lips. And she realized that she would miss Astrid very much.

Somehow she had gotten the feeling that Broadway shows that had run for a year would go on forever. Her own experience had been mostly three week runs. Anything longer than that became a part of life, like the routine of brushing one's teeth. She conjectured how long her own show might run. And when it stopped, what then?

"We'll drink to old lang syne, or something," Astrid said. "If you ever move yourself and get that bottle out."

"We have no quinine water."

"The faucet'll provide."

Ivy had no choice. She didn't feel like explaining how things were with her and alcohol. It would throw a blight on what had happened between them.

"I'm rather on the wagon now," Ivy said, letting her glance fall away from Astrid's amused expression. "Would you mind terribly if I didn't join you?"

"Whoops, how formal we are today." Astrid's shoulders rose in mock horror. 'Of course I mind. Who wants you to sit there stark, raving sober while I go tootling off?" She touched Ivy's chin with a flick of her forefinger. "We won't let you get sick, I promise."

Ivy didn't believe a word of it. And she didn't want the discretion she had so nicely arranged between herself and Drury to be shattered. She got a fresh bottle out of the case and prepared Astrid's drink, wishing that Astrid would stop looking at her long enough to notice the statues.

Astrid took the glass and bolted down the gin. "Stubborn little girl, aren't you?"

Ivy smiled. But she was watching Astrid drink and feeling the taste of it vicariously. She really could use something to pep herself up. "You haven't noticed my latest acquisitions," Ivy said, moving her breasts out of Astrid's reach.

"Oh?" Astrid commented, looking at her obscenely.

"No, these." Ivy picked up the sculpted hands and brought them over. "Like them?"

Astrid's eyebrows went up a little as her attention was caught. "They're splendid," she said. "Get them at auction?"

"I have more too." Ivy passed around the room, pointing them out. She had to struggle to keep her pride from making a nuisance of itself.

Astrid got up and followed her. "You never told me you go in for this sort of thing. I must say, your taste agrees with mine very nicely."

"Would you like some of them, Astrid?"

Astrid paused and took a speculative moment, tasting her gin and considering the enthusiasm confronting her. "I didn't know I was in for a tour of the gallery," she said.

Ivy became flustered. She wished Astrid would say whether or not she was willing to buy. But she realized that her own interest in Mike's work was, at this moment, out of proportion. Astrid could not possibly guess the reason for her deep interest.

She came over and put an arm around Astrid's waist. "Novices are bores, aren't they?" She wanted to be friendly and equally casual.

"Depends what they're novices at," Astrid chuckled. "Did you have a good time in Connecticut?" she asked with sudden sharp intuition.

"I'm afraid I was drunk as the Lord."

"Then you must've had a ball."

"No." Ivy stared back at Astrid directly. "He sobered me up quick, let me tell you. That newspaper item followed me clear up to Darien. I wasn't about to take a drink in celebration." She recalled the shock of it and shuddered internally.

"So that's the reason for this dry spell." Her words were half statement, half question. "I hope it didn't frighten you too much. We all get a taste of dirty words now and then. Like vitamin pills, you know. Keeps us on our toes."

They had seated themselves on the couch and Astrid had the bottle.

Ivy watched the window curtains flap. Night came on more and more quickly with each passing day. She saw it move across the sky beyond the broken line of spires and roof tops. Twilight had never depressed her so much as lately. She wished she could pull the fiery ball of sun back into the sky. It was terrible to be sitting here fencing words with Astrid. She felt as though their friendship was muddying. And soon Astrid would be off for California. They might not see each other for years. Ivy felt that she and Shepard and Drury and herself and Mike were like lead balls in a pinball machine, suddenly all to be shot out at the same time and go rolling away in their different directions, to fall into unpredicted pits and never be heard from again.

"I guess I'll take a sip of that," Ivy said.

Astrid handed over the bottle. "All yours."

Yes, it was all hers, the needing and the torment and the not-knowing. Mike would take his own sweet time about getting around to her. If ever. She raised the bottle and drank hard.

"Whoa, Silver." Astrid reached over and took the bottle down from Ivy's lips. "You don't want to overdo it."

"Don't I?" She was beginning to feel a little reckless. "Why not?"

"Because you might fall flat on that beautiful nose of yours when the curtain opens. I wouldn't care to read about it."

Ivy shrugged. She felt that Astrid was exaggerating. She had no intention of getting drunk. "Let's try not to be morbid."

Astrid tipped herself toward Ivy. "Confidentially, my dear, I had every desire to share a delightful hour with you." She laid her mouth in the hollow of Ivy's throat.

Ivy wanted to push her away. But she knew it meant pushing away their friendship too. The warm lips felt pleasant against her skin. Comforting to be wanted by someone, after Drury's rejection. "You don't want to reform me, do you, Astrid?"

"Heavens, what for?" The words drawled breathily.

Ivy draped her arm across Astrid's back, satisfied that one person, at least, was willing to take her for what she was.

She touched the close cut hair that molded the shape of Astrid's beautiful head, wishing they could stay close like this without getting intense about each other. But she knew that their warmth could not be held to a steady, low heat. Her own body needed to be held and fondled and told that it was loved. She lifted the bottle over Astrid's back and took another drink. Flames of desire began to arise. The desire which should have been satisfied by Drury.

Without prelude their bodies came together and held in a long, pulsing kiss. The words which warned her that Astrid could not satisfy her needs became blurred and distant. She felt the closeness, the life of another human being and Ivy didn't want to let go. It was like lying on a green hill in the sunshine.

Astrid's hands moved with a feathery touch. The odor of Lilac came from her skin, pleasing Ivy with its freshness. She could not think that this gentle intimacy was really disloyal to Drury.

They lay, half undressed and laughing at each other with the short, tense amusement of passion unveiling. Ivy caught Astrid's knee and placed it on her own hips as they lay on their sides. She thought they must look like a classic painting.

Astrid said, "Why are we always on the couch?"

"Are we?"

"Yes, haven't you noticed?"

Ivy wondered if it made any difference. "We could go any place you like," she said, anxious to please.

"Silly. I don't really care."

And to prove it, Astrid grabbed her ferociously, straining her ribs into Ivy's chest. She moved Ivy's thighs wide apart. "Gonna make you like it," she grunted with unconscious brutality.

Ivy closed her eyes and yielded. Images of men leaping naked from a high diving board crossed her mind in rapid succession. As each one hit the water with a heavy splash, her own body recoiled in shock. Faster and faster they jumped, flinging legs and arms into revealing poses. She felt herself hurtling through the air with them. The green water gurgled up around her ears. She caught her breath and held it till her lungs felt bursting. She seemed to hit the bottom of a pool in slow motion, then dream-like begin to rise to the surface.

Astrid was kissing her eyelids now and gradually regaining her own breath.

Ivy felt sadness instead of completion, though her limbs were relieved of a certain tenseness. She saw Astrid inspecting her closely.

"It doesn't work for you, does it?" Astrid said with gentle but scientific interest.

Ivy didn't want to lie. She shook her head. "But it's not only you," she added. "I have difficulty ... in general."

"Yes, I thought so."

"No cause for tears," Ivy said, trying to brighten. "I do have my moments now and then."

Astrid slid off the couch and flicked on a lamp in the gathering darkness. She lit two cigarettes and handed one to Ivy. "Whoever he is," Astrid said, "I know you'll get him."

Astrid kissed her again, but with a new undercurrent that told Ivy that she had a friend, a real friend, now.

They dressed and went to the theater.

# CHAPTER TEN

When Ivy arrived at the theater, she found a message to get in touch with Ed Denny. This brought her back to the responsibilities of her career with a jolt. She knew that Ed was not the kind of person to be considerate of one's personal life. He didn't have time and he wasn't interested.

She phoned his office immediately. Ed's secretary told her to come over after the show.

"I'll be there."

She would have to postpone seeing Drury and she sighed with disappointment. Anxiety to make up to him for this morning's disgrace would have to be controlled.

Three telephones were ringing in Ed's office when she entered, as though this were the day's start instead of its close. The evening secretary smiled at Ivy while continuing to type and told her to be seated. She spoke above the clacking keys in a well modulated voice. Anyone who worked for Ed could survive only by doing three things at the same time.

Ivy sat down gingerly on a dark wooden chair that might have come from the office of an old time dentist. She could hear Ed's voice bellowing into the phone. It came from behind a translucent door which partitioned off one corner of the drab tan room. There was certainly no glamour here to match the glamour of his famous clientele. Only stacks of papers and more papers shuffled about on the secretary's desk in a futile attempt at order. High in one corner, a small black fan whirred. The stench of cigar smoke pervaded everything.

In a few minutes Ed opened the door and jerked his head for Ivy to enter. He stood in his shirt sleeves, the dark gray tie hung loosely beneath the points of his limp collar.

He sat down on the edge of his desk, motioning Ivy to be seated in his swivel chair. A narrow window beside the chair looked out on the city.

"Is it true?" Ed got to the heart of matters quickly.

"The write up? Yes, it's true."

He picked up a dead cigar and knocked off the stiff, gray ash. "Okay. But that's the last time for you, kid. I got a nice young guy lined up. Hearts and flowers routine for the newspaper dogs." He felt around beneath the desk blotter and brought out a large sheet of stained paper. "Here's the schedule. Fit yourself into it and don't bother me."

Ivy recognized the boy's name. A new movie star, probably in New York between pictures. According to the schedule, she would be seeing him three nights a week for the next few months. The usual nightclubs, a play opening, a movie premier and two hospitals benefits. Precious little time would be left for Drury.

"You neglected to set the wedding day," she said acidly.

"Don't kid yourself."

She glanced quickly at Ed, then relaxed, seeing that he was simply responding in kind.

"So be nice," Ed continued. "You might even have some fun. He'll pick you up tomorrow at the theater."

With a wave of his meaty hand, she was dismissed.

Ivy folded the paper into her purse, anxious to speak with Drury about this and find out why, if she had to be seen with anyone, it couldn't be himself.

She had no patience for this kind of nonsense. Not right now, anyway. Dashing around town with a kid. Smiling plastic toothed smiles for greedy cameras. She needed all the time she could spare to be with Drury.

A taxi took her to his house.

Drury watched her with a touch of aloofness.

"I had to see Ed." She took out the paper and thrust it at him for proof. "What am I going to do? I don't want to spend my lifetime running around with a child."

Drury examined the paper and began to smile.

"It's not funny," she said. "If I'm going out, I want to go with you."

"That's very sweet, my dear." He tightened the cord of his lounging jacket. "But I'm a little too old for the romance mongers."

She had never thought of him as old. Her cheeks began to redden. "That's not true."

"I'm afraid you're wrong. Besides, it'll do you good to chase about. Skim off some of that excess energy."

She felt surprised that he trusted her. And then she realized that her own self-confidence was much too shaky for comfort. It wasn't that she objected to going about with a stranger. She objected to the opportunity it would give her to make a fool out of herself. After all, she couldn't very well sit in the El Morocco and drink milk. And there was no use pretending that she could get away with one safe drink. Supposing she swigged the stuff down and raped this youngster? How could she face Drury with a clear conscience?

"I've got to get out of this thing," she said, taking a cigarette from one of the inlaid boxes on the mantel.

Drury snapped the lighter shut. "I'm afraid you can't. At least you can't and still keep Ed."

"There are others."

"Yes. But none so good. And you'll find that all of them will expect you to bend to the love routine."

"Astrid doesn't," she said petulantly.

"Astrid is as old as I am ... if that's possible." He smiled to himself. "But look into her scrapbook sometime. See what they had going between herself and Shepard on and off for years. Who knows, maybe this Stack Highet will turn out to be another Shep Duncan. You want to help an up and coming actor, don't you?"

She was accustomed to Drury not giving in when she needed comfort most badly. Instead of arguing, she took one of the sandwiches that the Oriental had brought in and began chewing slowly. Perhaps Drury didn't want his name linked with hers. She knew very little about him, after all. A common interest had brought them together and a common desire had made them intimate. But she did not know what Drury thought about when he was alone. She didn't know what he wanted from life. Or from her, for that matter. And she had no claims on him. No guarantee that he must take care of her. Perhaps her vision of him was built on quicksand.

The food shifted uncomfortably in her stomach. She wished she could open Drury with a scissors and look inside to his deepest thoughts. For all she knew, Drury could despise her drunkenness and her indiscriminate sexuality. Why did she count on him? Her brief illusion of safety snapped off. In its place grew the spreading fear that she had trusted him too quickly.

Drury crossed his legs in a reading chair and tapped tobacco into a white meerschaum. "I've been thinking about your friend. The sculptor," he said with a blandness that made her wary.

Ivy put down the second half of her sandwich and wiped her fingers on a napkin. She tried to keep her face non-commital as the mention of Mike stabbed her.

"I've been thinking that he should study. Develop whatever potential there is under competent direction."

Ivy looked about for something to drink, pretending that her hunger and thirst were more important than Mike's future.

Drury went to the cabinet and poured her a glass of ginger ale. "I think you ought to speak with him. Tell him how you came into the possession of his work and suggest that he show his things to Bess Dublonsky. I'll be glad to introduce them."

Drury was standing over her now while she tasted the ginger ale, holding the glass tightly so that her fingers remained steady. She couldn't go to Mike. She didn't have what it took to face him and be impersonal. Her heart began to beat furiously. If there was any hope for her in this world, she had to stay far, far away from Mike.

"Bess is one of the finest in this country. And I'll see to it that she doesn't charge him very much."

Ivy saw that he was watching her carefully. How was she supposed to react? Why must she be the one to tell Mike? Drury could do it without trouble and save her the pain.

But of course this was nonsense. She herself was the logical intermediary. Her fingertips went cold and her cheeks hot. What was Drury getting at by doing this to her? He certainly didn't care about Mike.

"I don't think he would like my meddling," she said weakly.

"You mean you're afraid to see him."

The glass seemed to be slipping from her fingers. She guided it to the table. "Yes, I'm afraid," she said. She grabbed Drury's hands and clung to them. "I don't want to get involved again. I'm finished with him. You know that. I don't want anything to do with Mike. I want to be with you, Drury. I want the chance to straighten myself out and to be good for you. Can't you understand?"

He disengaged her hands and took the pipe from between his lips. "That's what I want to find out, Ivy. How do you think I feel when I come to you and find you rolling in gallons of gin? Do you think I say, she's just an old lush? I know better. And I know that nothing will ever work out for us if that bottle of alcohol must always be there. It's no different from having Mike right beside us in our bed."

She had never seen Drury become emotional. It frightened and pleased her at the same time. He did care. So much so that the thought of Mike was intolerable to him.

"Do you think it will help?" If Drury said yes, she would believe him.

"When you get thrown from a horse, the best thing to do is climb right back on …"

The particularly apt comparison made Ivy smile. Drury was right, as usual. She could not go through life being afraid to see Mike. She must go to him, speak to him as a friend and nothing more. Gradually she would learn to accept Mike on his own terms. Then, perhaps, she would not have to annihilate herself with gin.

"Is it possible?" Ivy finished the thought aloud. "Is it really possible?"

Drury gave her another sandwich. "My dear," he said with kindness, "We have no alternative."

Ivy decided to see Mike that very night and get it over with while her courage remained. She accepted Drury's offer to drive her downtown. He would wait for her in a nearby cafe. Her first impulse was to ask him to come upstairs with her. But this would defeat the purpose. She had to go alone. Tell him about Hilda, reveal her greediness to own his sculpture and throughout it all, maintain the platonic relationship so necessary to later success with Drury.

For the first time in many days, she was rock sober. The torture of seeing Mike choked up in her throat as she climbed the stairs. Her palm left wet prints on the bannister. Supposing she found Hilda there now? Supposing Mike would hear none of this talk about Bess Dublonsky? Beyond her self concern, she desperately wanted Mike to accept the offer. She prayed for the intelligence to explain to him and make him agree to see this Bess Dublonsky.

Instead of opening the door with her key, Ivy rang the bell. She listened to his brisk steps approach the door and stop precisely, as though he had counted them.

"Hello, Mike."

She saw his face puzzle swiftly at the caution in her voice. He was not surprised at her visit. No doubt he expected her to come, sooner or later. But this time, he sensed a difference.

"You sound like a funeral," he said, stepping aside for her to enter.

Ivy snapped the light on in the kitchen and waited for him to come sit down. He stood beside the refrigerator instead, one thumb hooked into the elastic of his pajama bottoms. His shirtless arms had a satiny glow, the naturally dark skin maintaining last summer's tan. With a supreme effort, Ivy averted her glance, holding a tight rein on the desire to run her mouth along those bare shoulders. With Mike, she didn't need a bottle. She needed only his hot breath, his tight grasp, his insistent desire racing with her own.

Against her will, Ivy felt herself rising inside, moving toward him as though at any moment her desire would leap out of her skin and across to him.

"I hope I didn't wake you," she said, faltering.

Mike opened the refrigerator and took out a container of milk. He pulled up the lid and drank from the container. "You woke me," he said, resting one arm on top of the door. "But I can stand it."

Ivy knew he was waiting for her to betray herself. To go to him and make him hold her. "I came to talk about something." She gripped her purse and hung onto it for ballast.

"No doubt." He was trying to break the spell of her formality. She could feel him straining to see her through the blindness, to be sure that her tone matched her demeanor.

"I mean your work," she added quickly.

"Oh?" He came to the table now and sat down. "What work?"

"Your sculpture," she said decidedly.

He drummed four fingers on the table, then let his palm fall flat. "I have nothing to say."

"But I have."

"You sound so goddamned peculiar." The words broke from him.

"Perhaps I do." She felt wrung dry with anguish. He was trying to reach her and she wouldn't help him. But it had to be like this. There was no other way. "I've come to talk business for once, Mike. And not ... anything else."

"Fine. So talk business. Maybe it'll go away."

"All right. It starts with Hilda, I'm sorry to say."

She told him the whole thing, sparing nothing except Drury's personal motive for sending her. Mike didn't have to know about Drury yet.

He listened without interruption but she saw the muscles in his jaw begin to pulse. He wasn't going to thank Hilda for what she'd done. Ivy hoped for one moment of pleasure that maybe he would get rid of her once and for all.

But when he spoke, it was not about Hilda at all. "I've heard of this Bess Dublonsky," he said. "And Drury Brent, too, for that matter. What I want to know is, why the hell should he give a damn?"

The old, defensive Mike.

"Simply because he admires your talent."

"Of course. And he admires your talent too, I'll bet."

"I'm not here to discuss Drury."

Ivy didn't want to lose her temper. She knew that once her guard was down it would fall all the way.

"What I want to know is why you had to come rushing here in the middle of the night for something so cold and impersonal. And don't tell me that Brent has nothing to do with it. An old lecher if ever I knew one."

"You don't know him at all. And besides, it's none of your business."

They both fell silent. Ivy's words hung startled between them. She had never spoken to Mike this way before. There was nothing about her that didn't concern him. She bit her lip and waited until the urge to apologize ebbed. It had been the right thing to say. Drury would be proud of her.

"We're progressing, aren't we, Ivy?"

"I have lots to keep me busy these days. It squeezed out nostalgia, if that's what you mean."

He felt around the table for a package of cigarettes. "I'm glad for you."

Ivy knew he meant this but she didn't know whether he liked it or not. She pushed the cigarettes to his hand.

"Well, I told you it would happen," he said, striking a match and finding the end of the cigarette.

Yes, he had told her many times. But she had never really listened. She didn't want to listen now. The only good sense she wanted right now was the feel of him pressing her into the mattress. Splitting her wide open, destroying her independence, making her part of himself.

"Let's talk about Bess Dublonsky," she said as he puffed clouds of smoke straight ahead at the wall.

"I get the message." He seemed to smile to himself as though a twist of irony had trapped him in a snare of his own making.

Yet she sensed, for no reason, that a burden seemed to be lifting from his shoulders. Had it been the burden of herself? The responsibility he felt to her? He could take her to bed without feeling responsibility.

"Will you see her, Mike?"

He pushed back from the table, tilting the chair on its hind legs. "What have I got to lose?"

She had been prepared for a battle and Mike wasn't giving her one. It was too good.

"Tell Brent, anytime." The words were like a challenge.

Ivy didn't want to press her luck. She had carried off this meeting well and she didn't know if her strength could sustain being with him now that she had run out of talk.

"You'll hear from us," she said, getting up and moving away. "I'll phone you to make arrangements."

She fled from the apartment and Mike's nearness.

The cold air bit into her cheeks as she rushed to the cafe and Drury. Her body was shivering from the sudden relaxation of control. Ivy felt as though she had just lived through a dream. Her insides slammed up and down, riding a roller coaster of near hysterics. She didn't know what she felt or what she wanted. Only to run, run till she bumped into something solid and real.

The smoky cafe was practically empty and she spotted Drury seated at the bar talking with the bartender.

She climbed up on the stool beside his.

"So you lived through it," Drury said.

"Of course. What did you expect?" She sounded ridiculous even to herself. The reflection of her face in the mirror behind the bottles was a taut pallid mask. She put her elbows on the bar and pressed the heels of her palms together, clasping and unclasping her fingers. She deserved a drink now, for good behavior.

"Gin and quinine," she said to the bartender.

He put down a towel and the shaker he was drying.

Drury grunted.

"Just one," she said to him. "You're having a drink." She felt peculiar needing an excuse to drink in front of Drury.

But Ivy knew she needed more than one drink and that she would get it.

"Well, did he accept?"

"Yes, he accepted," she replied a trifle belligerently. "All we have to do now is arrange the time."

"Very good."

Ivy swallowed her drink in large thirsty swallows, urging it to dissolve the feel of Mike around her.

Suddenly Drury paid the check and slid her off the stool. "You said one and that's all you're getting tonight, my dear."

For a second, Ivy held back, fighting him.

"Trust me," Drury said in a soothing voice.

It wasn't a question of trust. She wanted to go home and make furious love with him. Reassert the new Ivy Sherwood. But how could she let him touch her with the sound of Mike's voice still ringing in her ears.

Yet she went along with him, half afraid that if she didn't Drury would desert her. She had the crazy feeling that no one in the world really wanted her. That her body was a bauble to be played with for a night, then dropped in a corner.

They rode back to Ivy's apartment and she consoled herself with remembering the case of gin in reserve.

Her breasts felt like two smoldering hearths burning in the cups of her brassiere. She flung her clothes off when they got inside the door, not caring about modesty or deportment or how Drury might want her to act. She needed love quickly. She needed violence and rage and the destruction of her body that clamored crazily for attention.

Standing up, she put her legs around Drury's calves and pressed her hips tightly to him. She tried to enlarge the one drink imaginatively so that it would swell into ten and collapse the vise of dread gripping her in soberness. She inhaled the odor of liquor from him, making it part of herself. Drury … not Mike. Not Mike's puzzlement. Not Mike's thought that she was ceasing to love him.

She repeated Drury's name aloud and held it up to her own ears for conviction.

"Kiss me." She pulled his face between her breasts. "All over."

Wild strategy began to form in her brain. She would make him take her right here on the floor. Then he would be helpless and she could drag them both over to the bottle sitting beside the sofa. She put one of his hands between her legs.

"Rub me."

She felt his hand begin to search. He couldn't resist her passion. The sedate drama critic had his own set of weaknesses, she knew. And Ivy felt grateful that she could count on it. She bit his lip and forced her tongue inside his mouth.

Suddenly he lifted her off her feet and when she came down again, he had opened his trousers and gotten inside her. He walked her to the wall.

She stared over his shoulder to the bottle far away, hanging over his shoulder and pulling him tighter as she thumped her backside against the plaster. Their hips moved swifter in tempo. She strained to him, screaming high in her throat, knowing it couldn't happen but powerless to stop. Large beads of sweat slid down her spine. She reached around him and grabbed his tense buttocks, trying to swallow all of him into her.

"Harder, goddamn you," she moaned. She swallowed and the saliva seemed to run upward into her nose, burning and drowning her. She hit her head back against the wall wanting to smash the world to pieces.

"Put your hand there," he whispered. "Don't be afraid. Touch yourself."

She had no alternative. He forced her hand between them and her fingers began to move rapidly, becoming the agent of a stranger. In absorption with this, the presence of dread fell away. They slid to the floor and Drury hunched himself to give her room.

Her back began to arc upward, reaching a quivering peak. She inhaled her breath in a sudden gasp and then she seemed to burst open, her passion splattering like a ripe fruit.

Ivy opened her eyes. Her free hand reached up to touch Drury's cheek. She felt languid and amazed and wildly free.

"It happened," she breathed, not quite willing to believe the fact.

"Yes, of course," he said against her ear. "And we'll get better and better."

She placed her arms around his neck as tears of joy began to mingle with incredulous relief.

# CHAPTER ELEVEN

Stack Highet knocked on the dressing room door, introduced himself and thrust forward a white orchid corsage. He was the biggest man Ivy had ever seen, easily six foot six. His silver blonde hair, violet eyes and cleft jaw did a good job of covering up whatever he might lack in acting ability.

"I'm pleased to know you, ma'am," he said, as though speaking to a new born colt.

Ivy had spent the night lying awake beside Drury and trying to comprehend the wonderful thing that had happened. She felt very alert now and friendly to the whole world, as though she had just learned the pass word admitting her to human society.

"Sit down, Stack. I'll be ready in a minute."

He moved rangily in his dinner jacket, coming to terms with its formality by wearing a soft shirt underneath. He sat down on the edge of the trunk and waited. "I hope I'm not getting in the way."

Ivy was not accustomed to shy men. They'd never had the gumption to make out with her. She felt amused by Stack's apologetic attitude and wondered where he might rather be tonight.

"Not at all," Ivy laughed. "You have your orders." She finished applying the eye shadow, thinking that her face looked very well rested somehow.

"Want to pin the orchid for me?"

"My pleasure."

Up close he smelled soapy. And she decided he was harmless as a high school freshman on his first date. But this didn't deceive her. She felt the drive and the single-mindedness of him that had managed to crash the Hollywood gates. She knew how hard he must have worked to get rid of the Western drawl and learn to dance and to carry himself without the rolling, lockhipped stroll. Regardless of all the snide criticism she read in papers and heard from the outsiders, Ivy respected anyone who could stick it out in the acting profession.

"What's your real name, Stack?" She wanted to help put him at ease.

"Gideon," he said and grinned so that his polished teeth flashed. "Gideon Merckle, Jr."

"Mine's Isobel. They always called me Ivy for short, though, at home."

"Isobel. Ivy. They're both pretty names." He finished pinning the corsage. "I hope you'll call me Stack. You know, I still got to get used to hearing it."

"We'll practice."

She felt oodles of patience for him, this towering oak of a man. And it was nice not having to think, for a change. With Drury she needed all her wits and with Mike, all her self-possession.

They took a cab to the night club where Ed had reserved a table for them.

Ivy drank bourbon and water, pleased that she didn't need gin to bolster her. She listened to Stack talk about Hollywood and what life was like in the small town where he grew up. They danced a little and watched the comic slam his jokes across. It was a pleasant interlude for Ivy, giving her a chance to catch her breath between seeing Drury again and having to deal with Mike.

Ivy didn't know what to expect from herself now that she was a complete woman once more. She made Stack take her home early as the restless curiosity grew.

Alone in her apartment, she phoned Drury immediately. "I've got to see you," she said into the phone. "I want to make sure it's real."

It was real enough, he assured her. But he came over anyway.

"I spoke with Bess," Drury said between kisses.

Ivy couldn't let go of him. She felt experimental and anxious to make it happen again. Somehow, she didn't quite trust her one experience. What, for example, would have happened if she had let Stack in for the night? Was she capable with every man? Or just with Drury?

He got her hands out from beneath his jacket and sat her into a chair. "Will you listen to me for a moment?"

She didn't want Mike to intrude on her now. Wherever she turned, whatever she did always related back to Mike. Because of him, she was being an actress instead of a housewife. She'd been a lush and a whore and that was Mike's fault too. Everything good or bad or indifferent that happened to her, Mike was responsible for all of it.

"I don't want to hear about Bess," Ivy said, going after Drury and putting her arms around his waist. "Tell me that you love me."

Drury smiled. "You know I love you. It's a strange thing to happen to an old man. But I'm glad."

"I wish you'd stop saying that." It depressed her when Drury spoke about age. He couldn't be more than fifty. There were plenty of good years ahead. "Promise me you won't say such things ever again."

"But you can't push it away, darling. I want you to think about the difference in our ages carefully. Quite carefully." He kissed the bridge of her nose.

"If you're going to get morbid, I'd rather talk about Bess Dublonsky."

She had meant it to be a joke, but she saw that Drury was in no mood. He seemed more serious tonight than usual. But now wasn't a time for gravity. The world sat bright and beckoning in the palm of her hand. Why wouldn't he enjoy it with her?

"All right, we'll speak about Bess first." He disengaged her grasp and went to the window, shoving his hands deep into his pockets. "You can tell Mike he has an appointment with her next Tuesday. That's a week from today. At ten thirty in the morning. We'll pick him up and take him over." Drury leaned against the window frame and gazed down at the traffic. "I'm rather looking forward to meeting this Michael Devlin."

"You know something?" Ivy mused. "He's rather looking forward to meeting you, too."

She felt as though she were standing on a balanced seesaw between Mike and Drury. If she took a step in either direction, the balance would break and send her crashing.

With sudden decision, Drury came to her. He took her to the couch, sat her down and held both her hands tightly in his own. "Ivy, are you happy with me?"

His question was demanding. "Why should you ask that, my dear? You're the only one who can make me happy." She laughed to cover her nervousness. "Don't you know it?"

"I want to know it. Because I believe it's true. Oh, I don't expect that you're head over heels for me. But we have something better than that, don't we, darling? Something true and good."

Ivy waited, poised for she knew not what.

"And you know how deeply in love I am. Maybe your crazy dependence on me turned my head. But I don't think so. After all these years of knocking about, I've found what I've been missing. And I don't want to lose it. I don't want to lose you, darling."

Ivy felt the blood rushing toward the pit of her stomach. "What are you trying to say, Drury?"

He folded his hands together and squeezed them. "I want you to marry me," he said softly. "Right away, before we get sensible and let the moment slip by us."

Ivy caught her breath and tried to remain calm. She had never let herself think of anything so permanent with Drury. Of course she loved him. She really did. And their age difference didn't in the least concern her. Why shouldn't she marry him if he wanted her? Constancy, a strong hand to guide her. He would keep her on the right track and out of trouble.

But a niggling voice rose in argument. Mike would make a go of his sculpture. He was changing already. More sure of himself. In a few months he would be out of his shell altogether.

"I don't know what to say." Ivy freed one hand from his and passed it over her eyes. She was beginning to feel faint.

"Then say yes," Drury urged. "The time is now, Ivy. Surely you must know that. If we wait, we'll go on waiting. And," he added gently, "what is there to wait for?"

She looked up into his wise face. Drury knew very well what she was thinking. And he wouldn't ask her again. She felt positive of that.

"You must stop killing yourself with useless hopes."

It was true. Drury for a husband would make her sane again. She had promised herself to stop running after Mike. There was no good in it for her. Drury was right, as usual. And if she valued herself at all, she would act maturely now. Do the intelligent thing for once. Keep Drury by her side forever and have a fine, fruitful life with him.

She lifted her face to him, smiling with hope and sadness. "Oh, thank you, my darling," she whispered, closing her eyes and letting their lips touch ever so lightly.

"We'll get married the first of next week," he said. "Then you'll be safe. And all mine."

Ivy's brain began to spin. He was choking Mike off from her, forcibly, brutally. She thought: The next time I see him, I'll be Mrs. Drury Brent.

The idea was incredible. She felt herself drowning in an ocean of turmoil.

Never to know. Never to share Mike's success. But why must she keep hope for something that should have happened years ago? She had given Mike plenty of chance. Laid herself at his feet.

No stupidity, no desire, no love could make her keep on crawling to him. Somehow she had managed to struggle up into the light of independence. She could not slip back now into the dismal sickness of crying for him in the dark. Drury had helped her become a different woman. She was already beginning to conquer the fears which had paralyzed her. What insanity could make her want to return to gin and roaming the streets?

"Anything you say, Drury. I love you."

# CHAPTER TWELVE

S HE ROAMED the house numbly after he had gone. Now all the decisions were made, her fate directed, her destiny settled. If only she could relax and accept the inevitable. A gray hand of misery glided over her brain. Without thinking, she took out a bottle of gin from the case and sat down with it. Drury couldn't possibly mind if she got drunk alone. One last act of self-annihilation before settling down to the responsibilities of respectable wifedom.

Ivy unscrewed the cap and let it roll across the floor. On impulse she switched off all the lights and sat in the darkness, watching the curtains undulate before the partly opened windows. Her eyes gradually became accustomed to the darkness. A sliver of yellow from the street lamp cut a swatch across one of the dragons in the carpet. She took a deep breath and lifted the bottle to her mouth, wanting to empty it all in one gulp. The searing liquid spiralled through her chest and settled with a slow boil. She stared at one eye of the dragon, waiting for the misery to crumble and blow away.

Mike would split his guts when he found out what she had done.

"Good, you bastard," she said aloud. The sound of her voice rang strangely. "Goddamned, lousy, no good..." She paused, searching for stronger, more satisfying language while she pulled hard again from the bottle. But she could not find a word ugly enough to describe her feeling.

She pushed her shoes off and folded her legs under her behind. The high arms of the chair seemed to surround her. She wanted to sink deeper and deeper into the cushion till she disappeared. Her skin was beginning to warm up as she continued to call Mike names aloud in her head. An urge to get him on the phone and say them directly into his ear consumed her. She would tell him he was a lousy lay. Wouldn't *that* make the great Mr. Devlin flinch!

She finished the bottle and lit the stub of a cigarette from a nearby ash tray. Who needs you? I've got Drury Brent who really knows how to do it.

All of her seemed to glow with a need to flaunt her vengeance at Mike.

I know what I'll do. I'll go right down there and make believe I came to tell him 'bout Bess schmuckhead. Yeah, that's smart. Then very accidental like, I'll say—oh, by the way, honey pie, there's gonna be wedding bells next Monday. Come and bring a present. Heh, heh.

The idea couldn't wait. She toppled to the floor and crawled around in the dark searching for her shoes. She could find only one. Ivy put it on and hobbled into the bedroom for her purse.

But the elevator man refused to take Ivy down. Tactfully he cajoled her into returning for another shoe and perhaps a coat.

All right, if that's the way he wanted it. She got another shoe which almost matched in height of heel. She thought the black and brown combination was rather dashing. Both black would look like a funeral and make Mike suspicious.

The elevator seemed to bounce madly and she pressed herself against the wall till the doors slid open. The doorman got her a cab and steered her into it. All the way downtown she hummed busily to herself, anticipating how she was going to cut Mike up. Nonchalantly, of course. Very *savoir faire.*

Ivy rang the doorbell in three rhythmic spurts, then began to rummage for the key in case he was sleeping and didn't hear her. Mike wasn't going to hide from her tonight. She was going to give it to him all back. Right in his lap. Dump the pain and let him hold it for a change. Goodbye, Michael.

He opened the door as Ivy was trying to fit the key into the lock. She nearly toppled into his arms. But she caught herself and straightened up. His face looked kind of fuzzy and out of perspective, as though she were looking at him in a Coney Island funny mirror.

"How j'do." Ivy flicked her wrist and sauntered in. "I hope I am disturbing you." She hiccoughed and covered her lips with her knuckles.

"Whooee," Mike inhaled her breath.

"You won't smell a thing," she said. "Not a thing."

"I suppose that proves something."

"You can just take your hands off me. I'm not yours to hold." She wriggled herself away.

"I'm not sure I get it," Mike said. "You never used to be much of a drinker. Now you even make the papers."

Ivy flounced into the living room and bounced onto the couch. A large mound of plasticine stood with a damp towel draped over it beside an arm chair. She lifted off the towel and wiped her forehead, then replaced it carefully. "I didn't know you kept up," she said.

"Oh, you're a very exciting character."

"You can quit the sarcasm, old boy. I am exciting. Everybody gets excited by Ivy Sherwood."

Mike sat down on the divan beside her and leaned his arm against her thigh. "You're a real mess, my friend. Would you like to tell me what's happening?"

Ivy pulled her leg away and tucked her skirt tighter under her knees. "I didn't come here to discuss my private life. You may remember that it isn't any of your business."

Mike wasn't impressed. "You're so goddamned phoney," he said. "Why don't you spit it out and get it over with? Or is Brent your only chum these days?"

Ivy wanted to spit it out and right into his eye. But she hadn't built her news up to its proper climax yet. She wished she had another drink. Her heart was jumping like a buoy in a storm. Anger and disgust and hopelessness trumped her prize of revenge.

"Yes, Drury's my friend," she said. "And that's what I came here to tell you."

"That Drury's your friend?" he laughed.

"No, stupid. He made the appointment with Bess Dubl … Delbl … you know. Tuesday morning. Ten thirty."

"And that's why you're here and filled stinko to the gills? Tell me another."

He was being much too difficult. In fact, he was stealing the fun right out of her grasp. She jabbed the heel of her shoe into his hip. He caught her foot and held it fast.

"You let go of me," she said in a low cold voice. But she didn't feel cold. She felt volcanic.

"Not till you tell me what's wrecking you."

"Look who's talking. How long did you sit in this lousy dump …"

"That's over with."

Ivy stopped suddenly. She didn't know what to say. "That's good. And lots of other things are over with too. Now let go of my foot."

"You won't kick again?"

"I don't have to kick you. I don't even know why I bothered to come here. Coulda called you on the phone. Maybe I thought you'd like to hear it from me in person. For old time's sake. Or something."

She waited for this to sink in. Mike took a piece of clay and began to roll it between his palms. "Go ahead."

"All right, if you're all calmed down." Ivy balanced herself on one elbow.

"I said go ahead." His voice was impatient and harsh.

Inconceivably she began to feel frightened. "Well now," she hesitated, wanting to grab that infernal clay out of his hands and fling it against the wall. "I am about to ... become a bride."

She had never heard herself sound quite so idiotic.

"You what?" He twisted around and stared straight at her. His eyes glittered with disbelief and seemed to pierce her own with perfect, focused vision.

Ivy slid herself into sitting position and put the pillow on her lap, clutching it tightly to her. "You heard me."

"Say it again."

She felt that Mike was daring her. He had no right. This was her show ... all hers. With a sudden icy flow of emotion, she hated him.

"I am going to get married, thank God," she repeated.

"You're lying," he said flatly.

Ivy smiled now, feeling the return of self-confidence. Tight lines had etched into the sides of his mouth and he was grinding the edges of his teeth together, waiting for her to deny it. She watched Mike suffer, enjoying herself with an almost frenzied delight.

"I am not a liar. I am a truth teller. Tomorrow I shall have an engagement ring and Monday I shall have a husband. If you promise to wear a carnation, you may come to the ceremony. Monday morning at City Hall. Nine o'clock sharp." She didn't actually know what time Drury would arrange it for, but nine o'clock sounded definite.

"I'm sorry. But I can't believe you, Ivy." He squeezed the clay flat between his hands. "It doesn't make sense."

"It'll make sense, all right. When I have that plain gold band on my finger." Her voice sounded large with truth.

"If that's the case ..." But he didn't finish the thought. "Well, who's the lucky man?" His voice sounded a little tired, a little annoyed.

"Oh, I suppose you can make an educated guess." She wanted him to dangle for a while on the point of her pin.

"No, I cannot."

"Think about it." She folded the pillow in half over her arm. Maybe now, Mike would know how she felt all those months and what it was like to come in and find Hilda.

"Not your famous theater critic."

"Yes. My famous theater critic," she mimiced his tone.

"You're insane."

Her hand shot out and whacked him across the cheeks. She saw the red fingerprints begin to blossom. "Insane, am I? I'll be a damn sight better off than I ever was with you. He uses his brains. And considerate? Drury knows everything about me. He's sweet and understanding and he loves me. He tells me that he loves me. With him, I don't have to sit around and wonder what's going to happen next. I've got my pride, Mike. Whether you like it or not. You want a floozy running after your tail, my boy, and I'm not the one for it. Not any more, I'm not. There comes a time when you have to grow up and face yourself. And that's what I'm doing now. No more of this living for the moment and crying into my beer about the injustice of fate. I've had it, Mike. I'm through with you and you better know it."

Ivy bounced off the couch and tried to stand evenly on both her feet. The balloon of anger was all fizzled out now. She felt a little sick. A tremendous blob of fatigue sagged down from her shoulders through the length of her spine. She looked at Mike for one last minute, watching him slowly squeeze the clay out at either end of his fist.

She wanted to kiss him, just for a second, without him feeling it. But there would be no more of that in her life. Not forever.

She got his key out and let it fall with a tiny plink into a copper bowl.

"Goodbye, Mike," she whispered in a sudden breath of tenderness.

Then she propelled herself blindly out the door.

# CHAPTER THIRTEEN

URING THE next few days, Ivy felt as though she were living inside a cellophane wrapper. She could look out on the world and be aware of what was going on, but she could not really touch it. She told herself that this sense of unreality would go away in time. Just a matter of becoming accustomed to new habits. The habit, for example, of wearing Drury's ring.

He'd bought her a black star sapphire instead of the usual diamond solitaire. When Ivy pulled her gloves on, the large stone caught and stretched the leather uncomfortably. When she washed her hands, the ring slipped around to the inside of her finger. It was a beautiful stone and she admired Drury's taste. Yet it seemed to weigh down her hand annoyingly.

She knew she should phone Ed and tell him of her coming marriage. There was no point in going out with Stack anymore. The publicity would only complicate matters. But she couldn't bring herself to lift the phone.

And she certainly should call her folks. They would put her through a long inquisition about Drury. Then she should bring him to the house for dinner.

Ivy made a mental list of all the loose ends which had to be tied up before Monday. She started to go about them like a robot responding to buttons being pressed.

Ed yelled so loudly over the phone that she had to hold the receiver away from her ear. He insisted that she should come down to his office immediately.

Ivy went. She knew there was nothing Ed could say that would change her mind. But so long as he was in charge of her career, she owed him the courtesy.

The day secretary was busy transcribing from a dictaphone. Her bluish gray hair popped out in defiant corkscrews around the metal head phone. Her fingers raced madly, jiggling the corpulent flesh in a neverending battle against time. Ivy saw the shadows of two other people in Ed's office. When they came out, she saw it was Colin and a pert brunette who clung to his arm as though she could not walk without his help. He kept Ed well supplied with new clients, Ivy thought while she nodded an aloof greeting. She had never imagined Colin on a treadmill. But in his own way, he was no better off than Ed's secretary.

In contrast, she felt privileged to have Drury.

"You come in here," Ed shouted.

She swept past Colin and his latest while they continued on their way out.

Ivy closed herself in with Ed, knowing that he was about to blast without caring if the whole city heard.

Ed stood behind his swivel chair, rocking it. "Repeat what you told me."

Ivy sat down on one of the straight backed chairs facing him. She was not going to let her own temper be whipped up. "I am going to marry Drury Brent," she said a little stiffly.

"Yeah, that's what you said. And I never heard anything so stupid." The unbelievable announcement had dissipated his anger. He did not know what to do in the face of such obvious self-annihilation.

"And you're going to quit the stage?"

Ivy had not thought about this. She did not want to give up acting. And Drury certainly would not expect this of her.

"No. I want to keep on."

Ed sat down now and tapped the point of a pencil on a sheaf of papers. "Then hold off for six months. There's a picture contract I'm looking to get you." He spoke with comparative calm.

"I don't see the connection," Ivy said, lighting a cigarette to ward off the odor of his cigars.

"You don't have to see any connection." Ed flung the pencil down. "You just do what I tell you. This is a lousy business and I won't have you mess things up by getting pregnant."

"Is that all your worried about?" Ivy laughed nervously.

"If I told you all the things that could go wrong at any one moment, you'd drop your teeth, kid. Now do yourself a favor and listen to me. Roll around with Stack for a couple more months. Believe me, I know what's good."

"I'd like to, Ed." She leaned across to his ashtray. "But I can't."

"Whatdaya mean, you can't?" He pushed some papers away with disgust. "Pregnant already?"

It wasn't an insult, but a realistic complication that might have to be dealt with.

"No," Ivy said. "I just can't, that's all."

She couldn't very well explain to Ed the shrewdly delicate timing which Drury had purposely arranged.

"All right, you can't." Ed pulled the chair closer to his desk. The wheels squeaked. "But you keep that fascinating lover boy home nights. I want to smear the magazines all over with marital bliss. Starry eyed goo to the hilt. You understand?"

"Yes, I understand."

But she didn't understand why Ed was picking on Drury. "You don't like him, do you?"

"Who doesn't like him? He's sweet to the photogs and publicity boys like a dog with rabies. Sure I like him." Ed patted his chest heatedly. "Far away from my business responsibilities."

Yes, it sounded like Drury. Drury was a closed circle unto himself. Uncooperative to newshawks. And why not? He had his own status and didn't need people like Ed. She felt proud of

Drury and glad to be part of his private interests. She rubbed out the cigarette.

"I'll do what I can, Ed," she replied, knowing that Drury was not going to give an inch.

"You're damn right you will."

Ivy came out of his office needing a cup of coffee.

It was Friday afternoon and she didn't know how a whole week could fly by so fast. She had better get in touch with her mother now, while Dad was still at the office. Easier to face them one at a time. Break it gently. Though what could they possibly have against her future husband? Ivy laughed at the misgivings which had been jostling her. She decided to have that cup of coffee with her mother.

The crowded apartment looked different somehow and it took a moment before Ivy realized why. Two bureaus and extra lamps which had broken and waited for years to be fixed had all been moved into her old room. The place was a little airier, easier to move around in.

"You don't sleep here anymore," her mother said. "So we're making use of the space. Maybe when Leo goes to college, he'll need an extra place where to study."

Ivy felt glad that her folks weren't waiting for her to come home. She was encouraged to tell her mother about Drury. She waited until they had toasted some white bread and were sitting cozily in the warm kitchen.

As she spoke of marriage, her mother's face took on a hopeful light.

"He must be a very nice man if you would marry him," she said. "We'll make a big wedding. I still got the linens that I was saving for you all these years."

Ivy let her mother talk and plan. Perhaps they would have a big wedding after the civil ceremony, if Drury would agree. All the friction between herself and her parents would die a quiet death. The future was rosier than a teen age dream, Ivy told herself.

"Dad will like him," she said.

"Oh, your father will love him like another son."

Yes, Ivy repeated in her heart, I've made the right decision.

"I'll bring him over Sunday."


On Sunday afternoon, Drury said all the right things to her parents. Everyone was eager to please every one else and the hours glided by without one sign of friction. Suddenly it was as though Ivy had always been a model daughter. When they left, her father kissed her on both cheeks.

In the taxi going back to her apartment, Ivy said, "How do you feel about it?"

Drury stretched out and crossed his ankles. "I feel wonderful about everything, my dear. What do you mean?"

"I mean a formal wedding."

"Would you like one?"

"Would you?"

They both laughed.

"Anything you say," Drury replied.

Ivy closed her eyes and sneaked her hand into his. "I couldn't be happier," she sighed.

They shut the door of her apartment and held each other close.

"Stay with me tonight," Ivy murmured. "I don't ever want to be separated from you again."

"Even if Ed tells you to divorce me because I'm no good for your career?" He said the words against her earlobe.

"The devil with Ed. I've got my darling." She swayed with Drury, pecking her lips all over his face.

"Are you hungry?" Drury said. "Shall I send out for dinner?"

"I'm hungry. But not for food."

"You should eat something."

Ivy slid her arms under his jacket and across his back. "I'd rather start our honeymoon."

He rubbed his palms over her ribs. "Wouldn't you rather wait till it's legal?"

"The hell you say," Ivy chuckled. "I could be dead by then."

They hadn't touched each other for too many nights and Ivy's flesh began to tingle with pent up desire. "Take my clothes off, darling. I want to feel you touching me."

She wanted to sprawl out on the dragons and smother them in her lust with Drury. "Here," she said. "On the rug." Her voice was growing breathless with anticipation.

"No inhibitions," Drury smiled. "That's what I like most of all about you."

They lay down on the rug and began to undress each other, massaging skin beneath underwear, kissing, inspecting, enjoying the special odor of body heat.

In languid abandon, Ivy stretched wide her arms and legs. Drury pressed his lips to her breasts and her body began to beat in a wild tempo. Her reservoir of craving bubbled up and spilled over. She climbed on top of him, pinning Drury to the rug with her hips. A sharp intake of breath tore from her as she straddled him.

"I'm going to pound you through the floor," she said.

"Mad devil."

She rode him hard and fast. Her perspiring thighs slipped against him. She came up almost onto her knees in the growing fury of action. What did she need? Only this man beneath her. She wanted always to be aware of him, feel him penetrating her with love, fertilizing her with his need.

Ivy rolled them over so she could have his whole weight on top of her now. She locked her ankles and swung to and fro against his chest. It was wonderful... perfect... the world outside be damned. She began to slide her hand between them, but Drury took it out again.

"Won't need that," he grunted.

Ivy felt him twist and insinuate himself even more closely. All of her felt open and flat against him.

"Up and down," she muttered.

Her body rocked on an ocean of flame. She stood on her shoulders to get him further in. Her back trembled and her breasts slapped together. A long feather seemed to be tickling her belly, goading her passion.

She flung obscenities, rolling them and tasting them round her mouth. Her jaws suddenly locked as a large convulsion overwhelmed her. It broke into smaller, tinier waves and died in a series of shudders.

"Oh, how marvelous," she breathed, wiping perspiration from beneath her eyes.

Drury found a handkerchief and blotted perspiration from her neck. "Anytime you need me," he said.

They crawled into each other's arms and fell asleep naked on the rug.

The doorbell rang and shattered Ivy awake. She got herself out of Drury's arms and struggled to sit up. He yawned and put his face into the crook of his elbow.

"Just a minute!" She shook him till he opened his eyes. "Go on to the bedroom," she whispered. "Someone's at the door."

His clothes were scattered all over the room and she threw them into the bedroom after Drury. Then she got her raincoat out of the closet and slipped it over her.

"Mike!" Her voice snapped on his name.

He held a long white cane with a red tip. "Why not?" he said.

She could not think or reason. Her body felt icy cold and paralyzed. But her mute, animal sense knew that he must not come inside.

Swinging the cane in front of him, he took long secure steps into the living room. "You never invited me so I thought..." He walked about, touching pieces of furniture, the cushions of the sofa. "I don't find any open suitcases," he said. "Shouldn't you be packing?"

"We aren't going out of town," she said, feeling the panic grow. "Drury has a job and I have the play."

"Of course. I should have remembered." Mike cocked his head, suddenly alerted. "Why doesn't Brent join us?" he said with a hint of aggression. "Or does he always hide in bedrooms?"

Though Ivy herself had heard nothing, she could not deny Drury's presence. She knew that Mike's ears were keener than those of sighted people.

"You're being obnoxious," Ivy said. "Mike, I wish you'd leave."

She could not bear to look at him. All her happiness, all her hopes for the future must be free from the threat of Mike.

"Do you?" He took a step forward and caught her wrist. His fingers hesitated as they touched the raincoat material. She saw his nostrils flare. He pulled her roughly to him and felt beneath the collar of the coat, finding her naked shoulders. "Does Brent always hide in bedrooms?" he called in a loud voice.

Drury came in, tucking the tails of his shirt into his trousers. "No, Brent doesn't," he said quietly. "Now take your hands off her."

Ivy pulled away from him. But she didn't move toward Drury. She felt as though she were watching two bulls about to gore each other and she moved away toward the wall without knowing it. She was breathing shallowly and very slow, though her heart bobbled and thudded in her chest. She could neither speak nor interfere on the behalf of either man.

Mike lifted his cane to a horizontal position and poked it about till he touched Drury's arm.

"You knew I'd be here," Drury said.

"No. I gave Ivy more credit. I see you've brain washed her thoroughly."

"Whatever Ivy does is no longer your concern." Drury spoke with conviction.

Ivy felt cold perspiration roll down her sides. She wanted to do something. But what?

"She doesn't love you," Mike said ferociously. He took a step toward Drury.

"You're quite wrong," Drury said. "But of course, I don't care what you think. It would be better if you went home. Before we have a scene."

"You're not going to marry her," Mike said from tight lips. His eyes blazed.

"Please ... go home and be a good little boy. You've caused Ivy quite enough distress."

Mike whirled, searching for Ivy. "You goddamned fool, where are you? Why don't you tell this bastard the truth? You love me and you know it."

Ivy couldn't speak. She trembled inside her raincoat.

"Tell him, I said!"

"She doesn't have to tell me anything. Ivy may have loved you once. But it's over with now. Finished. She can't stomach your egomania and your cowardice. I've shown her how to live as a mature person. From the looks of things, you can use a few lessons yourself."

Mike lunged and swung a fist, but Drury backed away with ease. Mike stumbled on the leg of a table and fell. But he stood up quickly. "If I had you ... If I could connect just once with that flabby chin of yours ..." His face drained to a pale white.

"I've lost a good bit of weight since the photographs you've probably seen."

Mike dug his cane into the rug. "Brent, I promise you ... you're not going to marry her."

"Fine. Now will you please go home? I'm sure Ivy is quite tired of all this."

"Bitch!" Mike flung into the air. "Stupid, foolish bitch."

Stumbling, he found his bearings to the door and let himself out.

When he had left, Ivy's head began to swim. She felt wretched with nausea and her throat burned. She collapsed onto the cushions of the sofa and hugged her knees to her chest.

Drury came to the couch and tried to put himself around her. "I'm so sorry, darling," he soothed. "Though you might have expected it. The boy has lost his main source of sympathy. I don't suppose one can blame him for ..."

"Don't touch me," Ivy said in a low, cold voice. She stared at the pattern of the upholstery, feeling far away from everything real and good. "I hate you. More than anything, I hate your filthy guts."

Drury laughed nervously. "You've had a shock," he said. "I'll make you some hot tea and put you to bed."

"No. You won't make me anything." She turned around now and sat up, huddling far away from him in one corner of the sofa. "I hope you rot in hell for what you did."

"I don't understand you, Ivy."

"How could you understand? You didn't see yourself the way I saw you."

"And what, precisely, did you see?"

"I saw a self-satisfied, puffed up imbecile. You treated him with condescension, you bastard. You treated him as though he were *pretending* he couldn't see."

"I don't like sympathy mongers," Drury said.

"Because you're deaf?" she said brutally. "Did the world collapse for you when you lost your hearing? Did it prevent you from making a big wheel of yourself in the career you had chosen? I doubt that very much." Ivy had stopped shaking now. She felt no sensation in her body at all.

"I'll get you a sedative," he said, straining for control.

"Get me nothing. I don't need a tranquilizer. I need to be alert to people like you. Sure, you would've married me. And made me a slave. Ivy can't make a decision without Drury. Ivy can't think without Drury. Ivy can't have an orgasm without Drury!" She hugged her shoulders, digging her nails into the raincoat. "Well, I don't know if it's true or not. But I'd rather drop dead this instant then be married to a pompous, unfeeling ..." She could not think of a description low enough.

Drury caught his breath. "You've said quite enough for one evening."

"I hope you understand every word."

Slowly he fixed the cuff links on his shirt. "Yes, I understand. And I'm sorry your mind is so distorted. But perhaps I should have recognized a hopeless neurotic when I saw one. The fault is mine. Misplaced optimism, I suppose."

"You can take your optimism and ... get out."

"So be it." He went swiftly to the bedroom and got his jacket. "I won't call you again."

Ivy dug her face into the cushion as the door slammed.


So this is the way the world ends .... Her mind jumped crazily through poems she had learned years ago in school. There was no future for her and the present was too miserable to live through. Better to dwell in the past for awhile, when times were innocent and men only boys who threw a snowball from behind a car.

She thought about getting up and spilling gallons of gin into the hollowness. But she knew that the empty feeling in her had no bottom. There could never be enough gin to fill it.

Ivy went to the radio and snapped it on, looking for a symphony to wrap around her. How incredible that there was life elsewhere. Only she was dead. Not dead, really. Alive with loathing. How close she had come to blinding herself about Drury.

Yes, it had been wrong of Mike to come here. But she thanked him for tearing the false clothes off Drury Brent. Neither of them would ever seek her out again.

Why hadn't she run to Mike when he challenged her love? But if she'd done that, it would have started all over again, the crawling to him.

She had changed in many ways during the past few weeks. But the total effect was single and complete. She had gained independence. However much her fear of loneliness pressed in, she did not need to flee blindly from sex. Or to it.

Of her own volition now, Ivy went to get herself a sedative. She needed to sleep somehow. There was a show to do. And the stage deserved her best.

When Tuesday morning came, she wondered about Bess Dublonsky and if Mike had ruined his chances. After Monday alone, she could think about him a little. Not too much and not too often. But enough to be proud.

It was nine o'clock. She scrambled eggs, put up coffee to perk and dropped halves of English muffins into the toaster. She thought about phoning Astrid to come join her. But Astrid would be too busy getting herself together for the Hollywood round. There was really no one to have breakfast with.

The doorbell rang and she thought that perhaps it was her mother bearing the bucketsful of consolation that she didn't really need. She straightened the gathers of her housecoat, determined to show her mother that all was really quite well. With a huge smile plastered on her face, Ivy opened the door.

"Mike." Her pulse skidded to a stop.

"*Miss* Sherwood?" His face was alive with amusement. He came inside and sniffed the coffee. "Am I in time for breakfast?"

"Mike, what do you want?" The smile had fallen from her face. Her eyelids felt as though they must be twitching.

"Breakfast, of course. I just told you." He found his own way to the kitchen and sat down, picking up a spoon and holding it expectantly. "You don't want to hear sad tales on an empty stomach."

She had to give him a plateful of eggs, pour coffee and butter the muffins.

"All right, I'll be kind and tell you. Poor Brent. I waited for him down in the lobby, as you might have known. But I didn't have to kill him after all. He stank from fear. I really was very ashamed of him." Mike's grin filled the room. "But so long as I just held onto his shirt, the words kept tumbling out. What you'd said to him and all." Mike took a long slug of the coffee and let out a deep breath of satisfaction. "I knew you had guts, little girl. Just took a while for you to learn to show 'em."

Embarrassment flared in Ivy's cheeks. "If you think you can take over where Drury left off, you're quite mistaken."

"Now, honey," Mike said. "Do you want to disappoint them down at City Hall?"

Ivy felt as though someone had sliced off her legs. She flopped heavily onto a chair. There were a million questions she wanted to ask. Petty little things. But what difference could they make when the biggest question of all was being answered right this living moment.

"An actress never disappoints her audience," Ivy said through tears she was glad Mike couldn't see.

He pulled his chair over to her.

His kiss tasted of butter and jelly and all the wonderful things that would go into their thousand tomorrows.